FOR SUSAN

D1247991

Prolog

The Mujahid ran the flat part of the razor-sharp blade along his palm and considered the best angle to slice through the traitor's neck.

The Mujahid stood behind the traitor, who knelt facing away. Thick hemp rope bound the traitor's hands tight behind his back. Sweat dampened his scalp and beaded the skin of his neck. He stank.

The Mujahid swiveled the *jambiya* sideways in his right hand, then with great care positioned its blade onto the traitor's right shoulder, the cutting edge facing away from the man's neck. The Mujahid would shed no blood before its time.

The traitor flinched at the first gentle touch of the knife on his shoulder. He began to tremble.

The Mujahid trembled too, but from anticipation. This was to be the Mujahid's first kill in America. Long ago on another continent far away, his great-great-grandfather had deployed with his own powerful right arm this same blade to spike an infidel Englishman in the throat. The Mujahid relished the honor of using his forefather's knife to spill blood here in America, in the very Citadel of the House of War.

The Mujahid had locked the traitor and himself into a tiny room barely more than a closet. The traitor's breathing came in short gasps, ragged and resonant in the tight space. Every so often he strained against his bonds and moaned.

Careful not to scratch any skin, the Mujahid lifted the jambiya from the traitor's shoulder, turned it in his hand, and pressed the blade up against the traitor's throat.

It was almost time. But Allah commanded the Mujahid to be merciful. Though the traitor had to die, he was not an animal; an explanation might yet help him find some crooked path to paradise.

"I know you are slow of mind, but I have prayed for you to understand this is for your benefit. It is your opportunity to make up for your sins. If you accept your martyrdom willingly, if you embrace death for the sake of jihad, you might still ascend straight to paradise. Do you

1

see?"

But the traitor was just as persistent in his iniquity as he had been consistent in his stupidity: "It wasn't a sin. It was just a mistake. There was no *niyyat*."

"As the Khaffir say, ignorance of the law is no excuse. And after you made what you claim was just a mistake, did you perform the mandatory prayers asking for forgiveness?"

The traitor contorted his neck, managing to edge it only a centimeter or two further from the blade.

"I thought not. Anyway, it wasn't just a mistake. You did what you did for money. You value money more than our jihad, and sex even more than money. So instead of hammering the hard drive into oblivion as I instructed, you just dumped the computer. I know all this. I even know where it went."

"I deleted all the files first."

"Your ignorance of the facts only compounds your ignorance of the law. You deleted the entries about the files in the hard drive directories. You had to wipe the data within the files completely. There are special commands for that."

"I didn't know about that."

In the Mujahid's experience, everyone knew about that. But ludicrous as it was, the traitor's claim was probably true. The traitor was an idiot.

So what? He had disobeyed. He had failed the first requirement—to submit. And his idiocy only rendered him a greater liability.

"All that doesn't matter. And now I have to track it down. This may delay our mission. We are here to bring Khaybar to America, not to chase after whores like Crusaders or after pennies like Jews."

"I can help with that."

"I can't trust you."

"This is not right. I am one of us."

"No. Now you yourself are Khaffir."

Back home the Mujahid had trained on animals. But he needed

little training. From the start he showed an intuitive knack. The knife movements came naturally. He always worked with determination and a steady hand that had earned him the warm praise of his teachers.

Later, after he had developed his skill in action in several countries, his commanders selected him for special preparation and ultimately this all-important assignment in America. He was ready.

Even so, his calm surprised him. He suppressed his trembling. His breathing came easy. His voice pronounced the words in a voice like a trained actor's: soft, mellifluous and evenly modulated. The words flowed naturally as blood.

He intoned the phrase "Allahu Akbar."

God is greatest.

Then it happened for him again just as it had happened for him so many other times in so many other countries on so many other continents. The joy rose from deep within his soul—the orgiastic pleasure he craved and had gone so long without. He embraced it. He savored it. He would do his duty and revel in every instant of the next few minutes.

Especially the screaming.

1   *First Encounter*

At first, Hack didn't know what to make of the curlicues:

خيبر

It was Thursday night. Hack was standing in front of his basement work bench, sucking down a cold beer while he tested the first of a trio of abandoned computers he'd salvaged.

The unfrosted ceiling bulbs cast hot white light and cool dark shadows. The buzz from his defective basement humidifier and the distorted guitars from his sound system melded into a hybrid music he enjoyed, if only because he thought this brand of heavy metal could be heard only in his basement and nowhere else in the world.

Hack stared at the squiggles and the squiggles stared back.

خيبر

Maybe it was a bug in the display. Hack turned the monitor off and on again. The squiggles reappeared. Could be some other component. He rebooted the entire system. But there it was again:

خيبر

He thought, Gus is right. I'm firing on at most two cylinders lately. That's writing.

Hack found a foreign language translation website. With the mouse he highlighted and copied and pasted the squiggles into the text entry box of the site. The site menu listed dozens of alphabets and even more languages to choose from. He tried Hindi, Thai, and a bunch of others until eventually he hit on Arabic, which returned:

Khaybar

Okay. "Khaybar." Pronounced how? Like "Kabar?"—his dad's old U.S. Marine knife, which rhymed with "day bar?" To distinguish this new word he decided to think of it as rhyming with "High Bar."

"Khaybar" rhymes with high bar.

"Khaybar"-a person, a place, a thing?

Hack had salvaged three computers from a pile of discarded equipment behind the local Ojibwa College Administration Building, where the administrators had stacked them—or more likely directed custodians to stack them. In Hack's experience, few administrators lifted or carried for themselves. For that kind of scut work they used lower echelon people, including occasional day workers like Gus.

Gus gave Hack a heads-up. "Take a look. You might be able to sell them. You know I got no use for computers, but if you make a lucky find, Little Gus will find a use for it."

Hack found the promised stack of computer components sitting forsaken and forlorn under that January's unusually gentle Minnesota sun, waiting to be carried off to wherever recycled hardware went.

Hack fit a laptop and the most promising components of two desktops into the back seat and trunk of the little red Audi Fox he was testing out for Gus and hauled them back to his basement workshop.

Hack loved to scavenge. So what if these discarded PC's poked along on low-capacity mechanical hard drives? Or their screens displayed only dim blurs for characters? Or their undersized memory bogged down trying to run the latest resource-hogging PC software?

The ones he couldn't resell at his shop he could give away. There was always a taker for a free computer. Plenty of local kids would be thrilled. No Ojibwa County farm worker—or even farm owner—enjoyed a fortune anywhere approaching the billion-dollar endowment Ojibwa College wallowed in.

And the more computers, the more opportunity to indulge his guilty pleasure: snooping through the secrets careless users had left behind on their unwiped hard drives.

Pursuing his shady hobby also gave Hack the chance to test out the newest version of a utility program for recovering lost data. Lacking much to do since his firing and the divorce proceeding, he had written the utility himself. He toyed with the idea of marketing it under it the name "Disk-Cover-IT," but like a lot of the schemes he started the past three years, nothing had come of it. He doubted anything would.

Gus had been blunter: "You won't do shit."

Hack's M.O. was to scan the first sentence of each document to see if it struck a spark. Once in a while he read on, like in the email a biology Teaching Assistant sent her professor boss:

> "Dearest Love Bunny,"
> "How long till I see you? When can I feel you inside me again? Why do so many conspire to keep us apart? Isn't there more to life than this? Why don't you answer my phone messages?
> "Love Puppy"

And why so many rhetorical questions? Hack wondered.

An Adjunct English Professor began her 40-page research proposal:

> "The proposed exploration will interrogate the hegemonic interface among peri-gender and peripheral heteronormative structures, leading to a discourse tending in the direction of peri-societal reconfiguration."

Hack felt no remorse spying on this gasbag—people who spouted this very same jargon had wrecked his career.

Another horny biologist or bonehead post-modernist was no big deal. But the Arabic word intrigued him enough to read more.

"Khaybar" was centered, and below it Hack found more Arabic text. He copied the text into the translation website and read:

> وسعيد محمد ،ومحمد جيش يهود يا خيبر خيبر يهود

> "Jews, remember Khaybar, the army of Muhammad is returning!

> "We met the Jewish workers of Khaybar coming out in the morning with their spades and baskets. When they

saw the Prophet and his army they cried, "Muhammad with his army," and turned tail and fled.

"Ali asked, 'Allah's Messenger, on what issue should I fight with these people?' Thereupon the Prophet said: 'Fight with them until they bear testimony to the fact that there is no god but Allah and Muhammad is his Messenger.'

"After the battle, the Prophet seized all their property. The Prophet ordered their warriors killed and their offspring and women taken as captives."

Hack thought, Nasty little tale. But don't judge without context. Hack hated both the behemoth "Google" and its search engine. Even more, he hated using "Privanation," the search engine he himself had written for his old employer Gogol-Chekhov, the company that had expressed its gratitude by canning him.

He searched via another search engine and found an additional explanation in English:

"The 'Khaybar' chant refers to the Muslim massacre of Jews after the capture of the Jewish village of Khaybar in northwestern Arabia in 628 CE. After the conquest and the massacre of the men, some Muslims, including Muhammad, took surviving Jewish women as wives. The Muslim conquerors charged the remaining Jews a 50 percent tax on their crops and in 637, after Muhammad's death, the Caliph Omar expelled the remaining Jews from Khaybar.

"The conquest signaled the end of all resistance to Islam in the Arab peninsula.

"This conquest also provided the occasion on

which the prophet Mohammed himself first uttered the phrase echoed by millions of jihadis since that time: 'Allahu Akbar'—Allah is greater--signifying that Allah is greater than any other people's god.

"Today, the 'Khaybar' chant is the rallying cry often heard at Muslim terror attacks against Jews as well as Islamist rallies and demonstrations:"

"Khaybar, Khaybar ya yahud"—"Jews, remember Khaybar, the army of Mohammad is returning!"

Likely this Khaybar story was part of some history course. All religions had their bombastic rhetoric and brutal pasts.

Judging by his name, Hack's next-door neighbor and friend Amir might be a Muslim, although Hack had never bothered to nail it down. Amir was a quiet sort who also lived alone. He ran the neighborhood convenience store. Two or three times a week, Amir dropped by to have some coffee and play chess or to come down the stairs into Hack's basement to watch Hack do his thing at the work bench. A couple of times Amir had brought his laptop over and Hack had straightened out some minor issues for him.

Maybe Amir could explain about Khaybar.

Like Gus said, Hack had nothing going. So maybe he was just looking for something to worry about. Even so, Hack doubted he would have bothered Amir about it, except that Hack's soon-to-be-ex-wife Lily and his never-to-be-ex-daughter Sarai were both Jews.

2 *Lunch With Lily*

"It's still not too late." Hack reminded Lily the next afternoon.

"Yes it is," Lily said. "It's too late today, it was too late when we had this identical argument last Friday, and it'll be too late when we rehash it next Friday."

They sat on opposite sides of a booth in Barry's Grill in St. Paul. They were waiting for the end of Sarai's week at the St. Paul Jewish Day School. Hack had made the 90-minute drive into town to retrieve Sarai and take her back to his Ojibwa City house for the weekend. He did that most Friday afternoons.

"There's no final decree," Hack said. He took the second-to-last bite of his turkey sandwich and a sip of his black cherry Soda.

"A formality."

Hack examined Lily for any sign of regret or doubt. Finding none, he tried a different tack. "I pored through every affidavit you wrote for the court. I took extensive notes. From the two minutes the custody hearing lasted, I could tell the judge never even glanced at them. So that makes me the only human being who ever read them."

She rewarded him with a small tight smile. "Thanks for the overdue attention."

"Did you really need seventeen?"

"I wrote them for me. It was the chance to straighten things out in my mind."

"I mention it only because it's a kind of validation to see someone still cares enough about me to carry so many intense grudges."

"Glad to validate."

"But the grudges prove we're still connected."

She leaned forward and propped her olive-skinned elbow on the table and cupped her perfect small chin in her tiny hand. The fall of her long dark hair framed her bright blue eyes. "Nat, we don't belong together."

"You thought different once."

"Things changed. You changed." Lily opened her left hand and began to count off on her its palm with her right index finger. "You developed the premiere software product for a fantastic startup. You were a rising star. Then you quit to run a crappy computer repair shop."

"I should put up with some nitwit ruining my work just because some other nitwit labels her diverse?"

"You put up with all the white male nitwits. I heard about every one in tedious detail. But for some reason this time you couldn't keep your mouth shut."

"Why start now?"

"But this time you had to quit?"

Hack discounted most Lily grievances and sympathized with some—he thought he knew a few of his limitations—but he hated this particular grievance. In the middle of all the humiliation, frustration and disruption of their divorce, he had never gotten around to telling Lily the truth. He never quit—they just fired him. His initial evasion had hardened into a brittle lie it was too late to recast.

"I just wanted to get away."

"To Ojibwa City?" She ticked off another count. "You ditched our great life together in a great town with great food, great restaurants, great schools, great social life, and great music so you could move to a tiny crappy house in a tiny crappy burg on the far edge of nowhere."

"I grew up in that tiny crappy house in that tiny crappy burg."

"It's still the fifties there. The eighteen fifties. I don't want to raise my daughter in that place. There's nothing for my career, and outside the College, no culture and no diversity."

"There's diversity."

"How?"

"Amir."

"Amir? Who's Amir?"

"My neighbor. We've gotten to be good friends, actually. Comes over all the time. He's a Muslim. I think. Maybe."

"From where?"

"One of those 'stan' countries. Maybe."

"You don't know what country your good friend is from?"

"Never came up."

"So there's a Muslim in Ojibwa City now? His life must be paradise."

Hack reflected. "Seems about like the rest of us—no more than normally unhappy."

"What's there for him to do there?"

"Runs a convenience store. Member in good standing of the Chamber of Commerce. Fits right in, as far as I can tell."

"I'll bet. But I'll let you have Amir, just in case."

"Don't forget the College. There's all different kinds of people there. Some are probably Muslims."

She perked up. "That's actually true. I know that for a fact. I just got a great new client who teaches part time there. Pays great too. He's Muslim. But he lives here in St. Paul."

Lily was a natural for the business she'd invented. Her father was the famous—or notorious—trial attorney Sam Lapidos. Sam's success generated a surplus of cash he lavished on his only daughter. Lily grew up awash in that cash. She absorbed fashion and style the same way Hack grew up knowing ballplayers and their statistics.

Four years ago, a friend had asked Lily's advice about how to dress for a presentation. A sales manager witnessed the stunning result and wondered how it happened. A rising executive from another company heard about her. Reference followed reference and she realized people would pay for the fruits of her spoiled upbringing. Her fees grew with her confidence and her reputation. She launched "The Lily Lapidos Enterprise."

As one of Minnesota's pioneer "image consultants," she shot to local fame with her breezy talk show makeovers. Hack remembered the weirdness of seeing his wife's face staring out at him from the cover of "Minnesota Happening!," a local glossy magazine.

Like her famous father, Lily left nothing to chance. She chose her clients' clothes and cars. She decorated their homes. She picked the right menus for the right social occasions and hired and fired the right caterers. She told her clients which clubs to join and which to quit. She decreed the correct restaurants to be seen lunching in as well as the wines to be seen sipping and the delicacies to be seen nibbling.

Hack asked, "And who's this great new client?"

"Tariq Daghestani. He's how I know there are Muslims at the College." Her expression suggested the most minimal possible grudging endorsement of Hack's crappy little burg.

Lily got that faraway look as she stared past Hack's shoulder into space. For the thousandth time he saw Sarai in her. Sarai was a miniature Lily, who—at barely five feet in heels—was pretty miniature herself.

Lily mused, "I think I'll go with the Sadiq Khan look."

"What's that?"

"Sadiq Khan. You know, the Mayor of London. Their first Muslim mayor ever. Tariq kind of resembles him." Her voice rose along with her enthusiasm. "So we'll go with warm colors, hair neatly trimmed and short, no beard. Always a dark suit. A very contemporary and very groomed image. And except formal occasions, no tie of course."

"Of course."

"Tariq's a very educated and sophisticated man. He's…what's the word?…courtly. Like from some high civilization and era long ago."

"When men were men and women were women?"

She sailed by. "There's so much suspicion towards immigrants now—especially Muslims. I told Tariq he's the kind of person can do something about that. And I can help."

"Sounds groovy." Hack took the last bite of his sandwich and final swallow of his soda.

She shot him a suspicious glance. She fell back on her customary approach to his minor provocations—she ignored him. "He knows lots of other really important people." She leaned against the wooden back of the booth. "I've been thinking about adding staff to help me out, but I can't for the life of me imagine who."

Hack gave a head shake in the direction of a solitary man in a nearby booth. "How about him?"

Lily glanced over to the man and then back at Hack. "What about him?"

"He's been paying us a lot of attention." It was true. The man made no attempt to disguise his scrutiny of the two of them, especially Lily. His gaze met Hack's unembarrassed.

The man's head was shaved, setting off the corded muscles of his neck. He wore a tight brown shirt that showed off many other muscles.

"Why him?"

"He's kind of middle eastern looking. Might be Muslim. Hiring him could do something more about that suspicion you mentioned."

"Don't change the subject," Lily said. "Where were we?"

Hack shrugged. Why help her keep on track?

"Oh. Right. Another thing. You studied all that music and all that piano and got a degree in advanced composition and then you threw it away. A man born with perfect pitch. Because one professor rejected one composition."

"Another nitwit. Anyway, I still play out."

"You play rock covers in a cheesy bar instead of your own compositions in a concert hall. Just like you peddle PC's instead of writing cutting edge software. And you even dumped your BMW—just walked away. You loved that car."

"You keep it. It'll burnish your image. It's high up on your list of approved vehicles, right?"

"I can buy my own car. And I saw you pull up in front of the Grill today in that clunker."

"That's no clunker. It's a classic. A 1973 Audi Fox Gus rebuilt. When I park people stop to admire it."

"People stop to gawk. It's a toy. Like your mini business and your mediocre band. You've totally lost interest in living a real adult life, which is what I want. It's like you sank into—"she stopped.

This was something new. "Into what?"

Her expression turned sad. "A torpor."

"A torpor?"

"Yeah. After you quit your job it was like you quit everything else too. When we met, you were bright and funny and engaging and fun to be with and then you went into this torpor. I waited two years for you to come out of it. But you don't. And that's why the divorce has to happen."

She continued, "Nat, I love you. More or less. You're a great father to Sarai, but you turned into a lousy companion to me." Her mask of cool had melted and a genuine expression of anguish appeared. "Can't you meet life at least hallway? Compromise?"

"I compromise. Remember, I went along right away when you wanted to raise Sarai Jewish?"

"Nat, it's not a compromise if you don't care. And you didn't care."

"I care. I want to see Sarai happy. And you too."

She smiled a genuine sad Lily smile and laid her hand gently on his. "Nat, we just don't belong together anymore."

Hack thrilled at any touch from Lily. He tried to ignore the electric feel of her fingers on his hand. "If you really want to compromise, you'll call off the divorce. We're still connected, if only through all your gripes. And through Sarai. And it's a mistake."

She withdrew her hand but the sad smile lingered. "Mistake or not, it's going to happen."

3 *Amir*

When Amir dropped over that night for their weekly chess game, Hack had two goals.

First, he was counting on Amir to reassure him that the Khaybar document was the world's biggest nothingburger.

Second, Hack wanted to avoid offending his friend. But Hack had no idea what would offend his friend from another culture on another continent.

He puzzled awhile and then decided the two had spent enough good times together. They were either friends or they weren't. He would bring up Khaybar in some natural sounding way and if it ticked off Amir, he'd learn something from that.

Hack was still sticking to his plan as the two men sat on opposite sides of the kitchen table, staring at the board. Amir was a short dark man who appeared to be in his late thirties. He seemed wiry and fit. He kept his dark thinning hair short. He had a small mustache he rubbed from time to time as he contemplated his moves. Amir had just touched his finger tips to his remaining bishop when Sarai emitted a sudden short buzzing sound.

Sarai had been darting in and out of the living room where she staged her toys in an elaborate pastime of her own invention Hack never understood. Every so often she dropped back to check on the game.

Now she stood staring at Amir, eyebrows up and head tilted in a cartoonish "hint hint" expression. She shook her head back and forth and buzzed with her lips pressed tight together.

Amir glanced at her. "What kind of noise is that for a modest young lady?"

She shrugged but kept on humming.

The two stared at each other a moment. Then Sarai caved into giggles.

"That's more like it," Amir said.

"But your move," she said. She shook her head yet again.

"Tell me again, how old are you?"

"Uncle Amir, you know. Nine."

"And at nine, you're already some kind of Life Master?"

Sarai sighed in sorrow. "That's so wrong. Life Masters play bridge. Chess is played by Grand Masters."

In the early months of their developing friendship, Hack had thought Amir shy and dour. When Amir did grant a smile, you had to earn it, and then it only flickered like a brief glint of sunlight on the blade of a knife. Hack had come to appreciate that rare smile. Sometimes he caught himself trying a bit too hard to coax it. But Sarai drew it out at will.

Amir flashed his smile now and said to Hack. "What have you done?"

"You're more to blame than me." Hack said.

"It's only the end game," Sarai said. "There's only five pieces left. How hard is that?"

Hack said, "Maybe it's an advantage to be younger."

"I'm not the only one she's younger than," Amir said.

Hack asked, "You going to make that move you were about to make, or has she warned you off?"

"It's not my night," Amir said, and tipped over his king.

"After the last two weeks, it was my turn," Hack said.

"Uncle Amir's position was hopeless anyway," Sarai said.

"You could do better?"

"Someday," replied Sarai. "After all, like you said, I'll keep getting older and bigger and smarter."

"So I better beat you while I can," Amir said.

Hack got up from the table to wash the dishes. Sarai took Hack's place and said what she said every time. "Maybe not this time, but some time, I'm going to win."

"Maybe some time. But not this time," said Amir. And he was right. But it seemed to Hack Amir let Sarai stay in the game a lot longer than he had to.

After the game, Hack put Sarai through her bed time

preparations. She changed into her pajamas and brushed her teeth and hopped into her bed in her room. He pulled her sheets and blanket up over her legs and body and leaned over to kiss her cheek.

"Hold it," she said. She pulled her big white stuffed bear to her side. "Now."

Then she said, "Dad, do you think Uncle Amir has a daughter?"

"Never heard him say. What makes you ask?"

"When I said good night, he called me 'Zahra'."

"Well, that's a lot like your name. Could be his accent. Or maybe that's Sarai in his home language."

She shook her head. "No, he said 'Zahra'. With a 'z'. Twice. He knows how to say an 's'. He says 's' all the time. And he called me Zahra last Friday night too. And the time before that."

"Really?"

"Don't you ever hear him?"

"No, but I'm happy you pay close attention to people. It's a good quality."

"And he seemed kind of sad when he said it. Like he meant something special. Could you ask him? I'd like it if I could have a cousin. The daughter of my uncle would be my cousin, right? I mean, even if he's not my real uncle. And she wouldn't have to be my real cousin. Or a boy cousin could be okay too, I guess."

Hack understood why Sarai would like to have a cousin, even if only a boy cousin. Hack was an only child and Lily was an only child and now Sarai was an only child. This all added up to no cousins for Sarai in any direction. Hack occasionally pondered the psychological significance of all that, if any, but he'd never come to any useful conclusion. He supposed the shrinks could, but he stayed away from shrinks. In fact, his many refusals to attend counseling had used up two entire Lily affidavits.

Hack said, "You're asking a good question, sweetheart. When I get the chance, I'll ask Uncle Amir."

He bent over to kiss her cheek. He felt her entwining her slender arms around his neck as she pressed her lips against his own cheek. When he straightened up she held on tight and as he straightened up he lifted her along with him. It was a joke she never tired of and she laughed as she always did. He kissed her again and gently pried her arms loose from the back of his neck as he leaned back over the bed. He dropped her smiling onto the softness of the bed.

He went to the door and turned out the light.

He heard her say, "Night, Dad."

"Good night, Sarai," and he closed the door.

On Hack's way back to the kitchen he found Amir sprawled on the living room couch watching Hack's television.

Hack sat on the easy chair next to him. "Something good on?"

"Local news. A friend texted me."

A dramatic horn fanfare blared from the TV. A dynamic logo flashed. A baritone pronounced, "And now breaking news!"

The local anchorman sported a lacquered dome of neatly parted brown hair. He also wore his most severe expression as he intoned: "An unusual murder victim was discovered early this evening in St. Paul on the banks of the Mississippi River. Jessica March has the report."

Microphone in hand, a young woman appeared on the screen. The January wind whipped her hair into her face and she had to keep brushing it away. Behind her, uniformed cops and others in suits milled around a hillside overlooking the river.

"Thank you, Bud. It's chaos here. The victim has been identified as Mohammad Abadi. Shockingly, he was beheaded."

Hack snuck a glance at Amir. Amir was impassive.

Bud asked, "Do the police have any leads?"

"All police are saying for now is they wonder who would commit such a gruesome crime. But the local community is already expressing its outrage. They want answers. Here's community leader Tariq Daghestani. He was a mentor to the young victim."

The camera panned back and the reporter turned and thrust her microphone in front of the man standing next to her. "Professor Daghestani, your thoughts?"

Daghestani looked as Lily had described him—a solid olive-skinned man about forty. Maybe Lily had already done her makeover. His dark hair was short and neatly trimmed and he wore a dark suit jacket with no tie.

Daghestani spoke a mildly accented but clear English flavored with Canadian-sounding vowels. "When I heard of this dreadful crime, my first reaction was horror. I knew this young man. I mentored him. He had a stunning future. Now some evil person or persons have robbed him of that future."

"Do you have any thoughts who that was?"

Daghestani shook his head. "None at this time."

"Do you see this as a hate crime?"

Daghestani said, "We can't know yet. Given the intense Islamophobia our community faces, we must consider the possibility. But first we will grant our police a fair chance to solve this crime."

"I've been talking to others in your community. They seem less willing to wait."

"There are always hot heads. We will urge calm."

The reporter turned to face the camera again. "There you have it, Bud. There are hot heads, but responsible leaders like Mr. Daghestani will be urging calm."

The screen cut to Bud's face again. "One additional development. At a previously scheduled event this evening, Governor Drebin took his opportunity to weigh in on the growing controversy."

Cut to Governor Drebin standing behind a lectern. "Would this have happened if Ahmed Abadi were not a Muslim? I don't think so. If there are second-rate Minnesotans who do not accept the presence of Muslims in our state, they should find another state. We don't want you here."

"What a tool," Amir said, He flicked the remote to turn it off. Then, "Did I use that word right?"

"Perfectly."

"I guess I shouldn't say that about your governor."

"He's your tool as much as mine. Feel free. This is America, right?"

"For now," Amir said.

Hack saw his opening. "You're Muslim yourself, right?"

"Of course."

"Does that murder upset you?"

"Doesn't it upset you?"

"Of course," Hack said. "And your religion is your business. I wasn't trying to pry."

"Pry away. It's time we did some prying. We've been hanging out for eight months and you haven't told me anything about yourself."

"Me?"

"You. You're pretty mysterious. Maybe even exotic. I move in next door to an empty old house and a few weeks after that you just show up."

"Nothing mysterious. I just want to live in my childhood home."

"And for that entire eight months almost all you do is come out of your house and ski around for a couple of hours and then you go right back in. You seem kind of"—Amir's voice assumed a gentle quality—"going through the motions."

"What motions?

"Of life. I don't want to offend you, but you're playing with old desk top computers in your basement when everyone tells me you're a computer genius."

"Genius? Where'd you get that?"

"What about your nickname—'Hack'?"

"Ah," said Hack. "That's not because I'm some kind of hacker. I got the nickname from baseball."

"How does "Hack" come from baseball?"

"I was a free swinger."

Amir opened his hands in the universal invitation to continue.

"I always took my 'hacks'. Swung at everything. High, low, inside, outside, no matter what. I didn't care. No impulse control. I was just a kid.

"And top of that is my build. That's why they made me a catcher. And there was this old-time ball player early last century. Hack Wilson. He was only five foot six and he weighed like two hundred twenty pounds. He perched this enormous bulk on little size six feet."

"You don't look that heavy."

"More like one-eighty—still a lot for my height. But this Hack Wilson was a great hitter. Set amazing records. I was playing ball in high school and one day I got lucky off this tough pitcher Andy Schultz—"Raggedy" Andy everybody called him—he got to Triple A but never made the bigs—and I tagged one and my coach who was a baseball historian type squinted me up and down and called me "Hack" after that old time player. The name stuck."

Amir raised his right eyebrow.

Hack said, "I guess I'm running on. Do you understand any of what I just said?"

"Sure. You scored a long-range screamer on a promising goalkeeper who ultimately ascended to a premier league team. Then your youth coach gave you that nickname "Hack" the way mine might have named me "Ronaldo" or "Pele" after the originals."

"That's about right."

"Revealing."

"You're a bit of a tricky guy, aren't you? Know how to get people talking. I've been angling to ask you a question and you've got me babbling about me."

"Revealing because you don't play chess like a free swinger. No wild moves or big sacrifices. Your game is positional."

"So?"

"You make these incremental moves. Look like nothing. Then your opponent all of a sudden realizes he's screwed."

"Maybe I've grown up."

"Or life has made you more thoughtful? The responsibility of Sarai to watch over? Bitter experiences we all face sooner or later?"

"Okay. You've accessed my semi-encrypted secrets. What about yours?"

Amir said, "If there's something you want to know, my friend, why not just ask?"

"Okay. Where'd you come from?"

"I came via France."

"Not what I expected to hear. I know you got here a few weeks before me. That's less than a year, right? But you speak English great."

"I learned English before France."

"Why?"

"People all over the world think it's an advantage to know English. And in general they're right."

"Lucky for you, I guess."

"Yes. Very lucky." But the way Amir said it sounded not so lucky. He added, "I also happened to get a lot of chances to practice with Americans in my original home, which was Iraq."

"Iraq. So if I show you something in Arabic, you can tell me what it means?."

"I can try. There isn't just one uniform Arabic language. There are many dialects and many versions spread over many countries on many continents. With my mother tongue, meanings can be slippery. Things are often said indirectly. Not so blunt and direct as our American English."

"I understand."

"Maybe you do. Or maybe you don't. But if all your questions are just stops on some roundabout path to asking me to read something in Arabic, you've skied all over town to get there. Why not just show me?"

"Sorry. You're right. It's in the basement." Hack stood and led Amir to the basement stairs and flicked the light switch. Amir followed him down the narrow gray painted wood steps and then to the bench. Hack switched on the monitor and the computer. The system booted up and they waited in silence. Amir seemed very good at waiting in silence. Hack envied that trait, since he had so often suffered the consequences of its lack in himself.

Hack found the "Khaybar" file and brought it up on the screen.

خيبر

وسعيد محمد ومحمد جيش يهود يا خيبر خيبر

يهود●

Amir peered over his shoulder. "Show me more."

"Take your time." Hack stepped away and Amir took his place. Amir scrolled down the document and back up again.

Hack asked, "So what do you think?"

"Where'd you get it?"

Hack explained and added, "I suppose it's just some history lesson."

"You don't know whose computer this was?"

"Can't say. I can't find a name in English. You see a name somewhere there in Arabic?"

Amir shook his head. "Though it's not a lecture. It's more like a letter."

"From or to?"

"Can't say. It describes accurately what happened about fourteen hundred years ago. But in Modern Standard Arabic, not the Arabic in which the events were originally recorded."

"Is that significant?"

"Might be." Amir didn't say why.

"You think it's just a blowhard?"

"A blowhard?"

"You know, someone talking a lot. Shooting off his mouth. Making a big empty wind."

Amir nodded. "Likely a blowhard."

"Lord knows there's plenty over at the College."

"No shortage of blowhards anywhere. So it's probably nothing. I always used to dismiss the blowhards myself. Then a storm came up and the blowhards blew away everything worth having."

He added enigmatically, "You saw the news."

Amir walked away from the work bench and slumped down on the ancient wooden chair in the basement corner. He stared at the floor at least a minute.

Hack remained silent and avoided interrupting Amir's thoughts wherever they were taking him.

Amir said, "Sarai goes to a Jewish school, right?"

"Sure."

"I don't want to scare you, but while I was in France, jihadi killers murdered Jewish school children. Those monsters chanted that Khaybar chant in exactly those same words: *"Khaybar, Khaybar ya yahud."*

"Thanks for not scaring me."

"I'm truly sorry, my friend."

Hack asked, "Is there some way you could learn more about that letter?"

Amir finally looked up at Hack. "I don't personally have anything to do with the College. But I might know someone willing to help."

4   At The Madhouse

Another Saturday night gig at Max's Madhouse. As always Hack came hoping to enjoy himself but found himself feeling he was just slogging through.

Hack and his band were working through their medley of Rolling Stones hits when Hack noticed the unusual dancer.

What made the dancer unusual was that he was good. The man moved with exquisite rhythm as he snaked his way in a sinuous strut. The stranger's feline stylings bore no resemblance to the stiff stomping, swaying and arm waving of the hard-drinking heavyset Minnesotans around him. He was a tawny cat slinking among a herd of earnest land tortoises.

Hack easily recognized him as the same man who'd been watching Lily and Hack in Barry's Grill the afternoon before.

From Hack's small portable stool he saw directly over his electric Yamaha keyboard. Although Hack heard nothing anyone said over the din of the band, Hack's spot on the band riser was the ideal vantage point. He needed no dialog. He anticipated every incidental bump or shove and every hoped-for hookup and every impending divorce.

Tonight their sometime lead singer Mattie had showed up to front the band, so Hack also enjoyed a great view of Mattie's butt. Mattie's nicely rounded rear focused his attention on the two fundamental facts of his current life: first, he was still married and desperate to stay that way; and second, he was still heterosexual, if only in theory.

Hack also got an eyeful—and every so often a faceful—of the long dark hair that fell down Mattie's back almost all the way to her tight blue jeans, as well as the many fascinating twists and turns those jeans made as she twisted to cup the mike in her hands and wailed in her powerful if erratic voice.

Hack's three instrumental band mates crowded behind him on the tiny riser. He felt a gentle nudge on the back of his neck and glanced back. It was the front tip of Gus Dropo's black Fender B-Pass electric bass.

Gus mouthed, "Keep your mind on the music."

Hack gave Gus a slow shake of his head in not-quite-mock despair and turned back. He didn't need to keep his mind on the music. His hands did that for him. They'd played every tune a thousand times.

The good dancer also took an interest in Mattie. He boogied his way up to the front, eyes on hers. She noticed and sang "Heart of Stone" right back. She bent down so her face was only a few feet from his:

"There've been so many guys that I've known

I've made so many cry and still I wonder why…"

Mattie turned to conduct the band through the final chords. She punched the air downward with her right fist. Then she swung around to face the cheering audience and take her bows, hair flying.

Homeless Hal took advantage of the moment and popped in front of the band stand. "Hello, Mr. Hack. Can I sing tonight?"

Hal was Ojibwa City's leading homeless citizen. He wasn't technically completely homeless, since townspeople took turns providing him decent places to sleep. Hack wasn't as generous as some others, but he did let Hal spend as many summer nights as he liked on the small screen porch in the back. Hack left a porch light on so Hal could find his way there on nights it suited him. He also left out a discarded sleeping bag he never planned to use again.

Mrs. Malkin was another benefactor. She let Hal sleep in her glassed-in back porch through the winter, which was why Hal had not frozen to death. She or others in her circle must have been keeping Hal in winter coats and boots as well.

Every Saturday night, Hal asked for permission to sing with the band. And every Saturday night Hack answered, "Sure, Hal."

Hal said, "Excellent."

"But let's have Mattie do one more."

"Also excellent." Hal stepped off to the side and clasped his hands in front of his big belly, an orange-bearded Buddha in a phosphorescent orange Gophers XXL sweatshirt.

Mattie belted out "Satisfaction" with even greater ferocity and to even greater applause.

Someone shouted "Hey, what about Hal?" Others joined in. "Hal!" They began to chant: "Hal! Hal! Hal!"

Cheers echoed as Hal stepped up to the riser.

Mattie gave Hal a sweet smile and handed Hal the microphone and curtsied out of his way.

Gus nudged Hack. "I think Hal's the only male human Mattie likes these days. Except maybe you."

"Me?"

Hal stepped up onto the riser. He was almost exactly Hack's height. He gave the impression he was more massive than Hack, but he wrapped himself in too many layers for Hack to be sure. Tonight he wore big loose dark blue wool pants patched in a similar-but-not-quite-matching blue—no doubt by Mrs. Malkin or one of her church friends. The white edge of his thermal undershirt poked out under the bottom edge of his sweatshirt.

Hal took up a lot more room than Mattie. The bulge of his belly swayed almost directly over Hack's keyboard when he turned around and asked, "Do you fellows know 'Jack and Diane'?"

Hal sang a repertoire of two songs, both by John Cougar Mellencamp. One was "Hurts So Good" and the other was "Jack and Diane."

Hal always asked that question as if it were his first time singing with the band. Hack couldn't tell whether Hal truly didn't remember or he just liked the ceremony.

As always, the band members nodded. Baz picked out the opening guitar lick. Gus and Hack and their drummer Mel joined in and Hal sang.

Hal leaned back like Pavarotti, hands cupped together in front of his belly and his tiny eyes shut. He paid no attention to the microphone. He didn't need one. His powerful tenor soared up to the black ceiling and rang round the room.

"A little ditty 'bout Jack and Diane,

Two American kids growing up in the heartland…"

A total transformation. Hal transmuted from seeming lost stumble bum to epic magic figure. He was a vessel music sang right through. He radiated unworldly power and clarity and beauty.

Hal boomed out the final notes of the song. He bowed once each in three directions towards the crowd and then once more back to the band. The roar rose higher. Hal beamed as he absorbed the sunshine and summer warmth of applause. A champion, he clasped his hands and waved them locked together above his head.

He stepped down onto the floor. People clapped him on the back as he made his way to the bar, where someone was sure to offer him a drink, which he was sure to turn down.

Hal was a teetotaler.

"Lips that touch liquor will never touch mine," he often declared.

Hack hoped there been a time in his life when someone's lips had touched Hal's.

The brief quiet that followed the storm of applause gave the good dancer his opening. "Drink?" he asked Mattie.

"Why not?" She looked at Hack.

"Break time," Hack said. "Go ahead."

Mattie announced into the microphone, "We'll be back in a few minutes," and then clicked it off. Mattie and the dancer headed together for the bar. Hack's butt was sore from its hour on the tiny stool. He stood up and stretched his arms up over his head.

Gus said, "I need a smoke."

Hack nodded and followed Gus out through the crowd and then through the back exit to the parking lot. They passed the two big black trash bins and stood at lot's edge in the bright light cast by the single lamp hanging high on its steel pole. They looked westward out over the back pond into the darkness of the barren fields and leafless January woods beyond.

Gus lit up a Lucky Strike and took a deep pull.

"I didn't know they still made Luckies," Hack said.

"Fifteen dollars a pack in the machine at Bingo's out by County

15."

"How do you afford that?"

"I can only smoke two or three in a day of these unfiltered jobs or I get a bad-ass headache. So it doesn't turn out all that expensive."

"Glad to hear it."

Gus blew a big puff of smoke towards the darkness. "Helps me keep the weight off," Gus said. "But you don't need any help with that, do you?"

"All my skiing."

"Partly, maybe. Have you eaten a single full meal since you moved back? Because I haven't seen it."

"Don't worry about me."

"That's the point, partner. If I don't worry about you, who will?" Then, "Did you notice the fancy dancer?"

"Sure. So did Mattie."

"Goes full circle. The dancer also had his eye on you."

"What do you mean?"

"He came by tonight before you made it in. When we were setting up. Asked if I knew you."

"By name?"

"By name." Gus flicked his Lucky into the pond. "Know why he might do that?"

"No idea. What'd you tell him?"

"I told him, 'I not only know him, I am him. Nat Wilder.'"

"Why?"

"Curious to see how much money you owe him."

"I owe nobody nothing."

"That's kind of the point of how you live these days, right?" Gus turned and inspected Hack. "So maybe you made some mistake some time or maybe there was some trouble I'd be better at handling than you, especially in your current condition."

"What condition is that?"

"You know. Indifferent."

29

"I prefer low-key."

"Passive."

"Relaxed."

"Inert."

Gus took out his cigarette pack and stared at it and then put it back in his pocket. "Do you ever come out of that cave of yours except to ski?"

"I play this gig."

"Which you sleep through. For all I can tell you've been asleep for the whole eight months you've been back."

"Please, Gus. Enough."

"Enough is right." Gus took out the pack again and this time removed a Lucky and lit it. "So this dancer? He's got a funny accent and I took an instant dislike to him anyway."

"Because of his accent?"

"You know me. I take dislikes. Often instant. Saves time."

"Amir's got an accent."

"Amir's cool. And now that you mention it, this dude's accent is like Amir's only stronger. But he's no Amir. I knew that on the spot."

Someone shouted and right away someone shouted louder. It sounded like they came from the other side of the Madhouse.

"Sounds like fun," Gus said, and took off. Hack chased him around the corner of the Madhouse building into the north part of the parking lot. The dark dancer was screaming at Mattie. His open left hand was lifted in the air. She bent over a few feet away with her back to him, her own left hand to her cheek, yelling in obvious rage.

Gus arrived ahead of Hack. "Hey!" he yelled. The dancer glanced his way.

Hack stopped just behind Gus and to his left.

"We don't allow that," the dancer said. The man's accent did remind Hack of Amir's, but thicker, as Gus had said.

"What's your name?" Hack spoke past Gus.

"What?"

"What's your name?" Hack had a theory that exchanging names

made potential antagonists into possible friends and reduced the risk of escalation. Of course, like most of his theories, it had limited practical application. "It seems there's been a misunderstanding."

"Call me Amalki," the man said.

"So, Amalki, has there been some kind of misunderstanding?" Gus asked.

Amalki repeated. "We don't allow that."

"Who's we?" Gus asked.

Amalki said, "We don't allow a whore to change her mind. Once she declares herself a whore, the rest is just haggling."

"Who's a whore?" shouted Mattie. Her black boot flashed forward and landed square on Amalki's shin.

Amalki backed up an instant and glanced at his pants leg. He cocked his right fist and stepped his left foot towards her. Gus's right fist hit flush on the left side of Amalki's jaw. Amalki went down.

Gus said to Hack. "You've slowed down, haven't you, partner?"

"I was hoping to avoid all this."

Amalki barely touched the pavement and was upright in a single almost acrobatic maneuver.

"So, Wilder," he said to Gus, "You like to fight?" With a deft move he slipped a knife out of his pocket and flicked it open. The five-inch blade glittered in the light. "I can make you as dickless as you act."

Gus snorted. "Dickless? You're the one just hit the asphalt."

"A man who won't control his women has no dick."

"Hold it." Hack stepped forward and raised both hands. "Just one misunderstanding piling on another. First"—he pointed to Mattie—"You obviously mistook our friend's intentions. Second, she's not a whore but third, even if she was according to local ground rules you don't get to hit her. And fourth, this man is not Wilder. I'm Wilder."

Gus said, "And fifthly, for your future information, around here we consider a man who hits a woman to be the one who's dickless. Which in this case is you."

"You're Wilder?" Amalki asked Hack. He seemed to relax.

"Then my work here is done." He turned again to Gus. "But I'll remember."

"That's why I did it," Gus said.

"One misunderstanding after another," Hack said. "Now you go your way and we go ours."

Amalki backed to his car. When he reached the driver door he yanked the driver door open, threw the knife in, jumped in after it, slammed the door, started the engine, backed out of his spot, and roared off into the darkness.

Gus said to Mattie. "What the hell was that all about?"

Mattie shrugged. "He's a good dancer."

Gus placed his hand on Mattie's face and turned it gently so that both he and Hack could see her left check. The beginning of a bruise purpled part of her face.

Gus said, "Let's go find him."

"Where?" Hack asked.

Gus's disappointment was obvious. "That's a problem, isn't it?"

Mattie pushed Gus's hand off her face. She glared at Hack. "You are useless."

"Hey," Gus said. "What about me? Don't I get to be useless too?"

Mattie turned and stalked towards the bar.

Gus said, "So we let that guy go? Not even any cops?"

"I don't think our kindly boss Max wants any more police reports from his parking lot."

"He'll get a fistful of police reports if Mattie doesn't get her divorce taken care of soon."

"Hey!" Mattie stood hand on hips in the light of the open doorway. "Get your asses in here. I want to sing."

The two men shrugged at each other and did as commanded.

5 Hunting For Khaybar

Sunday Hack made breakfast and then he and Sarai hung around playing various pretend games she devised. After each game she told him he'd lost. Since he never understood the rules, he was in no shape to argue.

Sunday night, Hack delivered Sarai back to Lily's place in St. Paul as usual. Also as usual, Sarai chattered away the entire 90 minutes from her child safety seat in the back. One snatch of conversation stayed with him.

"We had a great weekend, didn't we Dad?"

"Of course."

"We always do, don't we?"

"Sure thing."

"It's better than before."

"Better how?"

"Well, if you and Mom live in separate places, you can't argue, can you?"

Shows what you know. "That makes it a bit harder, I guess."

"And I like having two places to live."

"Glad to hear it." Although he wasn't.

She must have heard a hint of that in his voice. She added, "Sometimes, I mean. Just sometimes."

Monday morning he awoke to a tangle of sheets and blankets strewn about the bed and scattered onto the floor. Had he dreamed bad dreams? He remembered none.

After Amir's disturbed reaction to the Khaybar letter, Hack had to dig all the way through all three salvaged computers to see what more he could find.

He didn't feel like opening up the shop. He rarely did.

In order to mount the most effective search of the hard drives he needed to nail down what to search for. Hack spent Monday in his basement scouring the Internet for search terms. No beer this time—just coffee.

He found very few websites neutral on Islam. About half were Islamic sites proselytizing for conversion. A lot of others were hostile if not downright paranoid. Hack ignored the static and hunted for potentially productive search terms. He created a list of several dozen, including not only "Khaybar" but words like "jihad" and "sharia" and "quital" and "taqiyya" and dozens of others.

As he absorbed this new vocabulary Hack began to develop a general picture of Islam. He traced the life of the Prophet Mohammed in several versions. He discovered the distinction between the Quran and the Hadith and other holy writings. He learned hard-to-pronounce names of Muslim historians and commentators.

Hack read how Mohammed had married his final wife Aisha when she was six or seven and—according to the majority Muslim opinion—consummated the marriage when she was nine. He learned about Muhammed's death and the succession struggle afterwards between Mohammed's widow Aisha and daughter Fatima, as well as the subsequent bitterness and battles between Sunni and Shia that continue to the present.

Tuesday morning he had collected enough search terms. He began his hunt through the hard drives of the three computers. He searched not only for file names but also through all the contents of all the files for letter combinations.

The first time through, he used his personal hard drive utility DiskCover-IT. Then he did the same exploration all over again with a standard commercial utility.

On the old slow computers this part of his hunt took all Tuesday. He found nothing on two of the three computer's hard drives about Khaybar or any of his other search terms or even about Islam in general.

Late Tuesday night, he finally hit a small jackpot on the original Khaybar desk top. It was a single additional file in Arabic. When he tried the translation software, all he got back in English was gibberish. The words were unfamiliar to the translation software or for some other reason produced incomprehensible results.

He needed to show Amir. He printed both the Arabic version and the apparently failed translation. He checked the time. Almost midnight. Too late.

He went upstairs to bed. He set the phone in its charging cradle on the end table and lay down.

What felt like an instant later the racket of his ring tone shocked Hack half-awake. He sat up and rolled over and stretched out an arm to grab his phone. The time on it read 5:40 A.M..

Gus said, "You find those computers?"

Hack didn't waste words complaining about the early hours. "Sure, Gus. Just where you said they'd be. In fact, I've got two of them in decent shape. There's a laptop Little Gus might like. And by the way, good morning."

"I'll drop by tomorrow. Three P.M.?"

"Sure."

Gus hung up.

Hack rolled back over and tried for more sleep.

He had just dozed off when the phone jangled again. Hack rolled over and reached for it. About eight A.M. now. This time he checked the caller ID—suppressed. Hack pressed the "answer" button anyway and waited. No voice came. He gave it about ten seconds and then said, "Hello?" The caller hung up.

Back to sleep again.

No one else called. Hack finally lifted himself out of bed around noon.

He put on his coat and walked the sheets he'd printed over to Amir's house next door. No one home. He saw a note taped to Amir's front door: "Gone Skiing." Hack read the note as a personal message: as promised, Amir was checking out the Khaybar letter.

Hack returned to his house and made some coffee. He was sitting in the kitchen sipping it when the phone rang. He checked the caller ID and pressed the answer key.

"Say, Hack?"

"Hi, Mattie."

"How you doing?"

Hack censored his impulse to answer, "Still useless." Instead he said, "Fine."

Short pause, then "Could you do something for me?"

"Maybe." Caution paid in all things Mattie.

"That bastard Rennie took all kinds of my stuff. Even Toots."

"Toots?"

"My dog."

"Sorry to hear it."

"Nah—I hate that dog. Chewed up my shoes. He can have the bitch."

"Whatever you say."

Another pause.

Hack broke it. "So what can I do for you, Mattie?"

"He took our computer too. Can't get at my old email or any of that stuff. Plus I got to fill out some legal forms for the divorce. I hate using the phone with that peewee screen. You got one you could sell me cheap? Real cheap? This divorce has laid me low."

"Sure."

"When do you think you could?"

"I just got up. I'll have breakfast and bring something over right after."

"I got a better idea. You come over right now and I'll fix breakfast."

This was something new.

She said, "It's only fair."

Why not? "Okay."

"See you in an hour."

"What's your address again?"

She gave it to him and Hack shaved and showered and headed over. When he knocked, Mattie flung the door open and smiled a wide-open smile. Then she hugged him.

Mattie's enthusiasm caught Hack off balance. In school Mattie had always maintained a studied indifference to Hack. She seemed to tolerate his return to Ojibwa City, but he assumed that was more because he hired her for the singing gig at the Madhouse than any warm personal feeling.

He disentangled her arms from behind his waist and pushed her gently away, aware of the warmth of her bare shoulders in his hands.

She said, "Good to see you again, Hack."

"You've been seeing me for months."

"Yeah, but now I'm really seeing you."

"Whatever you say, Mattie."

"Come on in."

"First I'll get the hardware."

"I'll help."

Hack went back to the Fox and Mattie followed. Hack grabbed the computer case and Mattie took the monitor.

Mattie reached the front door before Hack and held the storm door open for him. The door led into a tiny kitchen.

"Not much space," she said, "But more without Rennie than with."

"Where to?" Hack asked, and Mattie took him into a small living room with a sagging dark green couch and an arm chair and a blond table. Then she led him through to her bedroom.

"That's fine," she said and pointed to a brown round table with a brown kitchen style wooden chair in front of it. He stuck the case under the table and she laid the monitor on top.

"Couple more things," he said. He went out to his car and got a box with cables, keyboard, mouse and power supply, then brought them in.

"I can set it up," he said.

She shook her head. "No, I'll take care of it. Besides, I promised you breakfast. Come on."

Back into the kitchen.

"How do you like your eggs?" she asked.

"You don't need to me make me anything. And I'm not hungry anyway."

"You're hungry."

"I'm not."

She made a show of casing him up and down. "I say you're hungry, all right?"

"I promise I'm not."

"Sit." She pointed to one of the two wooden chairs at the green painted table. "Please."

He sat in a chair and shuffled it forward under the table. The table was already set—two white plastic plates, tall glasses, grey metal knives, forks, and spoons, as well as a big clear glass jar with a screw top lid, filled to the top with orange juice. Condensation dripped down its sides.

Mattie bustled from stove to cupboard to shelf and back to stove again, humming some nameless tune to herself.

As the next fifteen minutes passed, Hack became increasingly conscious he had nothing interesting to say to her. But he felt no awkwardness. He might as well learn something from Amir and keep his mouth shut. He sat with both hands resting on the table before him, waiting for whatever was going to happen.

At first he made a conscious effort to ignore Mattie's jeans and what was beneath them as she swiveled her way around the kitchen.

But why bother? She made it clear she didn't care what display she made.

Hack told himself to relax. He wasn't in a Gogol-Chekhov cubicle any more. At GC a single careless word or wrong facial expression brought down the wrath of Human Resources and all the Inclusion Committees.

A woman had accused Hack's friend of "ogling." Not only did the poor bastard have to suffer interminable rounds of sensitivity training, but the transgression inspired a blizzard of memos extolling the virtues of diversity and their authors' moral superiority. According to the memos, hordes of retrograde male supremacists lurked in company cubicles.

Hack's final two years were an ordeal. People forgot that GC's actual purpose was to write and market software. Terror and suspicion made it progressively harder to do anything useful. Every meeting turned into a spectacle as ambitious recent college graduates paraded up to the lectern to outdo one another in parroting the latest diversity rhetoric.

Categories of the oppressed proliferated along with the corollary forbidden words about them. It was like a gold rush: social justice prospectors waved their nuggets of newly discovered oppression high in triumph and then hoarded them as treasure.

When Hack tried to focus more and more on what he considered his actual job, others noticed his failure to chime in. When a clique finally found an excuse, Hack's secretly documented "lack of commitment to diversity and inclusion" supplied the lubricant to grease his expulsion down the skids and out the door.

Obviously, nothing like that was going to happen in Mattie's kitchen. Did he really need to keep his head and eyes down at the table? Was he gawking at her butt? Did she care?

Mattie has a butt. She knows it. I know it. In fact, everyone knows it who's guzzled a single Saturday night beer at the Madhouse in the past six months.

Now that Hack granted himself freedom to conduct a more thorough examination, he spotted something else: no imprint of a bra strap under the cotton of her orange tee shirt.

She turned to glance back at him and confirmed his surmise—no bra.

She said, "Patience. Almost there."

"No hurry."

"I know. That's one of the things I've always liked about you."

"Never had a clue you liked anything about me."

She smiled an enigmatic smile and turned back to her work. With the flourish of a symphony conductor, she broke the eggs and spilled them into the pan and dropped the shells into a milk carton with its top ripped open. Then she scrambled the eggs.

A few minutes later she announced, "Here you are," and stepped to the table and began ladling out the goodies. "Your eggs, your home fried potatoes, your toast, your bacon, and your hot coffee, all arriving exactly the same time, hot and ready to eat. And don't forget the orange juice."

She sat down opposite Hack. "Timing is so important, don't you think? Everything coming together at the same time."

His voice surprised him and came out hoarse. "Thanks." How long since he had eaten a genuine home-cooked meal? Exactly as long since the last time a woman gave him food.

It turned out he was hungry after all. Hungrier than he could remember. He dug in with sincere enthusiasm. A few minutes passed before he remembered his manners and paused to glance up at her.

She had been watching him. She cupped her chin in her right hand. Her elbow was propped on the table. The weight of her chin in her hand raised the muscles in her trim right arm like small ridges on a three-dimensional map. Mattie looked as strong as a teenage boy, although Hack couldn't doubt she was female. Her long brown hair framed her lightly freckled face. Her strong nose endowed her face with more character than any conventional Hollywood prettiness. But it suited her. Her dark brown eyes regarded him with obvious amusement.

"Don't stop now, soldier," she said. "This is good for me too."

He asked, "Aren't you eating?"

"I already ate."

"Then why'd you make six eggs?"

"All this time I thought you were inspecting my ass and you were counting eggs."

"I can multi-task."

"Not according to Gus."

"Gus doesn't know everything about me." He paused. "I don't think."

He returned to the task at hand. Eventually he had to slow down, but he couldn't seem to stop while there was still food. He plowed his way through the six eggs and everything else. He cleared his plate and emptied the orange juice bottle for good measure.

He leaned back. He supposed he should feel sick. But actually he felt great. Maybe he'd get sick later.

"Don't forget the sweet roll," she said. She pointed to a cinnamon bun on a small white saucer.

"That's okay. Maybe in a while."

"There's no hurry."

"No, there isn't."

Neither said anything. Mattie seemed very comfortable.

Hack was not quite comfortable. He did not know for sure if there was a subject, but if there was, he felt a powerful need to change it fast. To some other subject as far away as possible. He broke the silence: "So."

"So."

"You remember that Amalki guy from the other night?"

"Sure."

"You haven't seen him since then?"

"No."

"Or heard from him?"

"No. Have you?"

"Maybe. Got some strange phone calls. Hang-ups. And I think I saw him once in St. Paul just the day before that."

"Haven't heard or seen a thing."

"Glad to hear it. But keep your eye out." He pushed his chair back and stood.

"Aren't you going to stick around for the sweet roll?"

"I don't think that's a good idea."

"Why not?"

"Well, I'm still married, you know."

"What's being married got to do with eating a sweet roll?"

"Nothing, I guess."

"Right." Her eyes narrowed. "Did you think something else was going to happen?"

"No. I mean…of course not."

She stood too. "Maybe you're right. It is time for you to clear out."

"Well, you know."

"No, I really don't know."

"My divorce isn't final."

"When's it final?"

"Any day, actually."

"I see."

"I hope I didn't make you mad."

"Why should I be mad?"

"So you're not?"

"No, but it is time for you take a hike."

"Should I take the sweet roll?"

She laughed. "Sure, Soldier, take the sweet roll. For the road. It'll be a while before you eat this good again."

Not a moment for inhibition. He grabbed the roll and wrapped it in his paper napkin. "So you're really not mad?" He put on his winter coat and his gloves and walked to the front door. He stepped through the storm door onto the stoop. He turned to say goodbye.

Mattie lunged forward and threw a skilled and powerful punch to his ribs.

Lucky his Minnesota winter coat was so thick—it was like being bashed with a brick. "I thought you weren't mad."

"Okay, so maybe I'm slightly mad. Or not. But I'm something." She searched his face. It seemed like she failed to find whatever she was after.

"I'll see you this Saturday night at the gig," he said.

"Yeah. That'll be nice." She stepped forward and shoved him in the chest and pushed him all the way off the stoop. He let her push him step by step backwards.

Mattie went inside and turned to close the door. Right before the door closed all the way, it paused an instant and he caught a glimpse of just the top part of her face, her eyes taking him in one last time. Then she slammed it the rest of the way shut.

Hack drove away feeling stupid.

Everyone in town knew Mattie was high strung and temperamental and dangerous to herself as well as others. That's why he'd kept his distance even in high school. Hack remembered a lot of times in his young male life when the deluge of juvenile hormones had flooded his brain and short circuited any normal caution or common sense, but none of those times had involved Mattie.

He wondered whether he was too beat down to know how normal women acted—all those years trapped in the chickocracy.

"Chickocracy" was Hack's private term for Gogol-Chekhov. His careless public use of that word had given the diversity queens something else to pounce on for their case for firing him. Allegedly the word made GC women feel they weren't safe.

Mattie doesn't expect to feel safe. She'll take her chances like the rest of us humans.

And if she doesn't like something, she'll dish out her own sensitivity training. She'll just punch me.

And she's hot too. And it's not just my natural raw horniness after months of deprivation. And it's not just her body, nice though that is.

Hack felt a stirring—something like excitement.—an urge he hadn't felt in months. For what? Freedom? Freedom like Mattie had?

Or Gus. To be direct. To act like who he was, which was male. To be stupid.

He wasn't sure whether he'd just now blown a chance to screw around. But if the divorce really did go through, the next time he got a chance to screw around, he wasn't going to screw around. He was going to screw around.

And she was hot too.

Really hot.

6 *Take Good Care of My Audi*

Thursday morning, 5:10 A.M. Hack's phone rang.

"We still on for this afternoon?"

"Yeah, Gus, we're still on. And good morning to you."

"Okay." Gus hung up and Hack turned over to try for more sleep.

A moment later the phone rang again. It was 7:40. The caller ID was blocked. Hack ignored it.

An hour later the phone rang again. Hack ignored it again. Again ten minutes later. Hack gave up on sleep and grabbed it and pressed the answer button. "Hello?"

"Is this Hack's Hard and SoftWare?"

"Who is this?"

"I drove by your shop yesterday but it was closed. Are you open today?" The voice carried a familiar accent.

"It's a slack week, but I can open up for a customer if I know one's coming."

"You are selective, I see."

"Say, do I know you?"

"Maybe. Do you?"

"You sound like someone I met the other night."

"You have good ears. From playing the music?"

It was Amalki. Hack said, "I don't think I'll open up for you. And don't come around."

"But we have things to discuss."

"No we don't." Hack hung up.

Hack got out of bed and carried the printout next door to Amir's house again. The "Gone skiing" note still hung on Amir's door.

By afternoon, Hack was down in his basement sipping a beer and trying again to make sense of the second document when a truck pulled up outside. A moment later he heard familiar heavy booted footsteps as Gus clumped down the steep stairs. A bottle of cold beer sweated condensation onto the big protruding knuckles of Gus's left hand.

Hack said, "Have you considered it might be risky strolling into people's houses and pilfering their beers?"

"You got no lock on the door, partner."

"What if I shot you?"

"You got no gun."

"You've got enough for both of us."

"The sad truth is there's never enough guns. And I don't think you could reach the Kabar in time. You'd have to break the glass." Gus stepped over to where Hack had framed his father's Marine Kabar combat knife and hung it on the wall. The knife shone through the glass with a well-oiled sheen.

Gus admired it a few seconds. "I've always liked your inscription."

Hack had taped below the display an index card on which he had hand printed, "In Case of Emergency, Break Glass."

Hack said, "I've got this glass beer bottle. I could break that over your head."

Gus grinned and lifted his own bottle. "Shall we duel?"

"Not today. I need you conscious. A problem with the Fox. And I have this for Little Gus." Hack pointed to a cardboard box with the salvaged laptop.

"Bring it on up. He'll like it. Show me the Fox?"

His occasional day work at the College was only one minor deal out of the many deals Gus always had going. His favorite was barter. Barter had many advantages. Gus's favorite advantage was tax consequences. There weren't any.

Gus was an off-the-grid guy who worked harder than most people just to avoid leaving any trail, paper or otherwise. "If they don't know what you're doing, they can't regulate it and they can't tax it. And they sure as Hell can't stop it."

Despite his highly developed technique, once in a while Gus accidentally did leave a trail. A few years previous, Hack had hooked Gus up with Hack's father-in-law Sam Lapidos to handle a scrape with the law. To Hack's mild surprise, these two men with nothing obvious in common bonded into instant buddies.

Today's barter was straightforward compared to the elaborate multi-party transactions Gus sometimes came up with. All Hack had to do was give Gus the laptop and Gus would take care of the rebuilt Audi Fox.

The Fox's history was murky. All Gus told Hack was "It'll run and don't worry about registration, license plate or tags. They're all taken care of. You'll be invisible, which you want these days anyway."

Hack led Gus up the stairs and to the attached garage and the Fox.

Gus regarded contemporary auto shops with contempt. "Triple R—remove and replace rackets." Gus never replaced anything he could fix and he thought with good reason he could fix anything.

The Gus approach worked especially well on the 1973 Fox because compared to newer cars it was simple and straight forward. Even Hack could lift the hood and recognize most engine components. The Fox regulated its mix of air and fuel with an old-fashioned carburetor, not with fuel injection. It ran fine with no diagnostic computer chips or for that matter any computer components at all.

"Pop the hood," Gus said, and Hack popped it.

The garage door rollers ground loud as Gus lifted the ancient manual door to air the space. "Start it," Gus said.

Hack got behind the wheel and started the engine.

Gus listened less than an instant. "I know your problem."

"Okay. What now?"

"Shut it off." Hack shut it off.

Gus said, "You got any epoxy?"

"Sure. On the shelf."

Gus went to the shelf, grabbed a flat bladed screwdriver, came back and reached in. "Come over," he said, and Hack did. With the screwdriver Gus pried off the distributor cap and displayed the cap. He left the cables still connected, one cable trailing to the coil and four to the four spark plugs. The cap looked like a small black five-arm octopus.

"Cap's cracked," Gus said. "See?"

"I see." Hack did.

"Hold it in place." Hack took it and held it.

Gus disappeared and reappeared with the tube of epoxy. He applied a small bit of epoxy to the crack.

"Get the hair dryer," he said. Hack got the hairdryer. Gus turned it on. "No heat," he said, "Just air. To dry it faster," and held the hair dryer to blow a few moments on the cap.

Gus clamped the cap back on the distributor and straightened up. He shut the hood gently. "That'll hold it for the drive to my place. I'll order a new cap and you'll be motoring around smooth in two days."

Hack said, "I'll follow you out."

Gus stepped outside. Hack got his coat and the laptop and got in the driver's seat and backed out the Fox. Then Gus pulled down the garage door and climbed into his pickup. He started off down the road. Hack followed in the Fox.

The drive was easy. The roads were still clear and dry in the rare snow-free January. They passed a few miles of barren winter farm land and then through the beginnings of the jack pine forest. As he usually did, Gus left Hack far behind, but Hack knew the way. He took the correct right turn up the long gravel road to Gus's place on the edge of thicker woods.

By the time Hack reached Gus's place, Gus had pulled to a stop in front of his garage and was walking over to the green shed nearby. Gus did his auto work in the shed. It was maybe fourteen by fourteen feet. Gus yanked the left front door open and then did the same with the right and went into the shed.

Little Gus came out of the white frame house and waved and then jogged over in his easy athletic gait. Back in high school his father had been the best athlete on every team—the best fullback, best shortstop, and despite his size, the fastest sprinter—all state all everything.

Gus had spent half a semester at the University of Minnesota and then returned to Ojibwa City. He'd never had any interest in academics and by then he'd lost all interest in sports.

Hack never learned what if anything had happened, but then he'd never asked.

Gus and Little Gus lived alone. Little Gus's mother was long gone. Little Gus was a clone of his father, a fifteen-year-old big for his age and already extraordinarily strong and fast for his species.

Hack pulled the Fox into the shed and climbed out.

"Hey Uncle Hack," Little Gus came in and started a contemporary juvenile greeting ritual involving trick handshakes and shoulder bumps and a few moves Hack couldn't follow. "Good try," said Little Gus. "Some day you might actually get it."

"Every time I figure out one set of moves, you change up."

"Gotta keep up with the times."

"Why?" his father asked. "I don't."

Little Gus grinned. "Well aware, Dad." Then, to Hack, "You here for the free beer as usual?"

Hack said, "Check the back seat, will you?"

Little Gus flung open the right rear door of the Fox and saw the laptop. "Very nice."

"See what you can do with that, will you?" Hack said. "I can't get much out of it."

Little Gus leaned into the car, grabbed up the laptop in his thick arms, and stepped back out. "Thanks. I'll see what I can do," and ambled back to his house.

"It'll take two days to get the new cap and install it," Gus said. "You'll be carless. That okay?"

"Sure. But I'll need to make the Saturday gig."

"You'll have it back in time for that with no problem. I'll give you a ride back today. But you better fortify first." Gus had an ancient faded blue cooler by the garage. He'd scavenged it from somewhere years ago. The big faded letters on the side read "*Miller High Life—the Champagne of Bottled Beers.*"

Gus strolled to the cooler and flipped up its silver colored lid. Rows of bottles glistening with condensation stood locked upright, their necks protruding through parallel metal bars. With practiced hand Gus slid a pair of bottles down to an opening where he could lift them up and through. He handed one to Hack. "I still get a kick out of getting one of these free."

The two used the bottle opener screwed to the side of the cooler, then walked over to the house and sat on the back porch steps and gazed towards the woods. For a while they said nothing. They took occasional belts from their beers. Gus took a pack out of his coat pocket and started to light up a Lucky and shook his head and stuck the cigarette back in the pack and the pack in his pocket.

Gus asked, "Heard anything from that Amalki dude?"

"As a matter of fact, just this morning. Got a phone call from him."

"What'd he want?"

"He claimed he wanted to buy a computer."

"And."

"No way."

"You wonder why he's taking such an interest in you?"

"No clue. I just told him to go away."

"You think he will? Didn't strike me at the time, but when I thought it over later, I noticed something odd about that dude—I mean aside from the obvious."

"What's that?"

"When I hit him he skipped right back up. Like it was nothing. Guys I hit usually stay down a lot longer."

"What do you think it means?"

Gus laid his big hand on Hack's knee. "It's probably a good idea for you to keep one of those beer bottles handy. You know. In case of emergency, break glass."

7 *A Romp In The Snow*

Hack and Lily had worked out a plan for Sarai to skip this particular weekend with Hack and stay in St. Paul. Something to do with some Jewish holiday coming up. In exchange, Hack could take the entire week with Sarai her next school vacation.

The Friday morning radio warned of a blizzard, but a glance out Hack's bedroom window showed nothing much coming down. He lay in bed all morning reading an old Travis McGee novel. Travis had infiltrated a wilderness terrorist training camp to avenge his lover's murder. He planned to wipe out all the terrorists all by himself. Hack was curious how Travis was going to accomplish that.

When Hack finished the book, he stumbled out of bed. A quick check out his front door showed him it wasn't even cold, so he didn't bother to put on his coat when he stepped out for his mail.

The sky was its customary Minnesota January gray. His yard showed ugly gray patches of gray dirt and dead brown strands of grass. A lone red cardinal flitting from one black leafless branch to another supplied the only vivid color.

Hack retrieved his mail from the box by the street and returned inside. Occasional light snow flakes began drifting down. When he stepped inside, he saw two of the standard credit card offers and a postcard promoting Ralph's Plumbing and the current week's issue of "The Ojibwa City Beacon," as well as one thick 13 inch by 16 inch manila envelope.

He didn't open the credit card offers or ads. He tossed them into the basket he kept for kindling. He put the big envelope on the kitchen table. The return address spelled all he wanted to put off learning—no hurry to open it.

He brewed more coffee and poured a cup. Still without his coat, he stepped outside again. He sat in the porch swing. For a while he watched the steam rise from the cup. A north wind began to cut through his thermal undershirt and whipped his unbuttoned flannel shirt around.

He sipped only two swallows of coffee and poured the majority out over the porch railing into his yard. As he returned inside, more white flakes danced in the air around him.

He opened the envelope and read the top page of the top document:

"In Re the Marriage of

Nathanael D. Wilder

AND

Lily Lapidos Wilder"

He sorted through the documents. The most important one took up just a few pages, and within those few pages, only one sentence mattered:

"The bonds of matrimony heretofore existing between the parties are hereby DISSOLVED."

For a while Hack sat at the table and stared at the outrageous sentence. He got up and crumpled the decree and threw it in the garbage can under the sink, but then he leaned over and lifted it out and uncrumpled it and laid it in the kindling basket.

Hack went to his bedroom and stripped off his jeans and his underwear and his white cotton tube socks. Butt naked from the waist down, he opened the bureau drawer where he kept his ski togs. He grabbed a bundle of gear and threw it on the bed.

He dug through the pile, then pulled on a one-piece thermal acrylic long blue underwear and over that a pair of briefs, then over those a pair of dark blue wool cargo pants. He yanked on an inner pair of acrylic socks and over those an outer pair of thick blue wool socks.

He took off his flannel shirt and put a tee-shirt over his thermal long-sleeved undershirt and then put the flannel shirt back on. He buttoned the top shirt all the way up to his neck.

He went out to the kitchen and opened the closet door. He retrieved his high ankle Gortex-lined waterproof winter boots and sat down on a kitchen chair. He laced the boots tight enough to fit secure but not too tight for circulation.

Hack walked into the garage and found his biggest back pack and stuffed it with a pair of ski boots, ski gloves, extra dry socks, underwear, an extra-large sweat shirt, trail snacks, his cell phone and two big bottles of water he filled from the garage sink.

He re-entered the kitchen. He picked up his kindling supply, including the divorce decree, then returned to the garage. He stuffed the kindling into his back pack. He put on his heaviest parka and then hoisted his pack on his back. He lifted his skis and poles, laid them over his shoulders, and stepped through the door. He began to walk away from his house and his town towards the woods.

The flakes were bigger and multiplying. A gale blew them into his face. He didn't mind. The stinging suited his mood. He kept walking.

He'd heard about an open flat place near a thick stand of woods where the predicted snowfall might lay down a base sufficient for skiing. He liked the idea of a new place to ski, especially one off the approved government-groomed trails. He focused on getting there. When he finally noticed that the wind and the snowfall were picking up, he felt a mild satisfaction. He kept walking.

After a while the snow was blotting out the sky—all white in all directions. Mounds of snow covered the ground. Even better.

He put up the hood of his parka and tied its laces under his chin and then drew on his mittens. He put on sun glasses to protect his eyes from the white glare. He kept walking.

He would know he'd arrived when he saw it.

After some indeterminate period he took a break. He had an idea the going would get rougher. He liked the idea of rough going—nature was delivering a challenge he was in the mood to enjoy—unlike the challenges people had been handing him lately.

He noticed there was now plenty of snow on the ground. He took off and lowered his pack and leaned against a tree to remove his hiking boots. He was careful to prevent his feet from making contact with the ever-deepening snow. He pulled his ski boots up and wriggled his feet into them and then clasped them tight. He leaned over to lock his boot bindings into his skis. He stuffed his walking boots into the pack and hoisted it onto his back again.

Now he could ski.

He headed towards those open spaces he'd seen on the maps—big flat places good for burning away his frustration and disappointment at himself and almost everyone else he knew.

The familiar hypnotic rhythm of arms and legs in counter-motion loosened and warmed him. Right leg swung with left arm, then left leg with right arm, then back again, over and over. An occasional change in movement broke the monotony. A few times he pointed his skis outward to herringbone up an uphill grade or tucked himself close to take it easy downhill. He especially loved coasting—it gave him an ease he felt he was earning as he went.

As he warmed he unzipped his coat and let it flap loose on his thighs, a welcome percussive accompaniment to his rhythmic leg and arm movements.

He focused on his motions, the easy swing and impact of pole in snow, center of ski gripping and pushing down into snow as he kicked forward. He breathed easy and relaxed. The temperature was perfect—cool enough he did not sweat much but not so frigid as to bite.

As the trees clumped closer together and the snow piled higher he kept an eye out for telltale bulges of buried logs and hidden tree roots.

After a few hours he stopped for a rest. He leaned against a maple trunk and snacked from his packets of trail food and guzzled a bottle of water. As he moved along, he stopped twice to relieve himself. He positioned himself leeward behind a thick trunk and bent to shield himself from the wind and to keep dry from his own stream.

To the extent he had any thoughts, time did not enter them.

At some point the sky had darkened from white to gray to near black. Night had come. Before him lay the edge of some thicker woods. Maybe these were the woods he was looking for and the open snow he wanted lay just beyond.

He stopped and gulped for breath. A wave of exhaustion washed over him. When he tried to start up again his legs were two stiff immobile chunks. His shaking hands could barely grip the poles.

The gale batted fist-sized chunks and lumps into his eyes. Through and beyond them he saw only snow falling in thick white sheets, all that was visible in any direction.

He thought, this is crazy. I've skied into a blizzard and I'm stuck in it. I need shelter.

But where? He spotted a huge dead log laying nearby on the leeward side of a mound on which stood a cluster of small trees which protected it from the wind and to some extent from the snow. He gauged the log at about three feet thick. Judging by the few patches of brown bark still visible through the piles of snow accumulated on and around it, it was a fallen oak. Its end might have been hollow. He crouched down and looked into an opening stretching inward several feet at least.

In the darkness he could not see how far. He stuck one of his ski poles into the hollow and felt only air. He looked around and found and hefted an eight- or ten-foot branch. He stuck it into the hollow, probing for width and depth. The branch moved freely. Plenty of room in there.

He lowered his parka hood and pulled his ski mask down over his face and then pulled the hood back up. The ski mask limited him to a narrow field of vision, but he could see nothing much anyway.

He felt an almost irresistible desire to sleep. With it came a warning to himself that this of course was hypothermia. He might be freezing to death.

No way to start a fire or even if he could to keep it burning. But he had heard of another way to keep warm outdoors on a winter night. The snow itself could insulate.

The blizzard is my friend. The blizzard is my friend.

He imagined himself chanting this in a sing-song voice, over and over, "The blizzard is my friend."

Or was he actually singing out loud? Not sure. If he was, it was lost in the overwhelming noise of the wind. That could be funny, or maybe not.

He took off his pack and took out two water bottles and stuck them inside his coat and zipped the coat up tight again. Bad idea to eat any of all that snow for hydration—that'd only cool his insides worse.

He lay the pack next to the log. He removed his skis and knelt down and then with care lowered his back down onto the snow, his feet pointed towards the hollow log. He propped his elbows on the ground and began to sidle feet first into the log. In a few moments he'd moved in almost all the way, sheltered to a point just above his shoulders. He reached out and pulled the skis in with him and clutched them close in his arms. He rolled over to face sideways, only his head poking out of the log, his parka hood shielding his nose and mouth and leaving a perfect small space for his own head to warm the air within that space.

The storm's arrhythmic sound began to soothe. It sang a continuous ragged pitched note, as if one single hit on a tambourine had been captured mid-rattle and elongated to an endless whirring noise. It was insistent and relentless and now that he paid attention surprisingly loud.

He welcomed the coruscating sound as a kind of natural concert. The musician in Hack embraced it as a minimalist composition—simple, repetitive and relentless. Although he'd never liked that minimalist music before.

He relaxed each body part one at a time. He started with his sore feet and then moved upwards to his tender knees and aching back and then to his neck, which was stiffening even as he tried to loosen it.

His musician's ear identified the storm's fundamental note—a D below middle C, with a descant of another D note soaring two octaves above it.

Of course, he thought. The First Movement of Mahler's

Symphony Number Nine ends on that exact D note. A fine note to end on.

8 No Place Like Home

Hack wakes to darkness, still safe inside his log. How long has he slept? The blizzard noise is gone. He hears something he's never heard: strange wails in the distance. Maybe they broke up his sleep?

Distant slow low pitched sirens begin at random intervals and then mingle and separate. They crescendo and decrescendo—louder and softer. Each wail rises and falls in its own distinct voice, each voice distinctly pitched. No recognizable harmony—the sounds simply collide one against another in a dissonant chorus.

Like somebody's tuning up to play. Or more likely, to sing. But singers don't tune up like that. Though maybe they should.

Then he gets it—wolves. For the first time in his life, he is hearing wolves howling in the wilderness.

Hack isn't the least bit cold. Buried in his log under the high-piled snowfall, he feels warm and safe as if he were tucked under his favorite blanket in his boyhood bedroom. He imagines his parents chatting downstairs with some visiting neighbors and cousins asleep nearby in neighboring rooms.

The wolves are locked out far away and anyway his mother and father will protect him.

An unexpected emotion—like an actual physical sensation of warmth—swells upward and outward from his deepest being and burns through him. He's still alive. He's strong and healthy. He's hearing wolves in the night.

The memory of his boyhood home reminds him he now possesses something he couldn't imagine then: a child of his own. A daughter as beautiful and alive and in need of protection as he was.

How could he fail to do for her what her grandparents had done for him?

He sees himself now not as a bold adventurer striding with purpose into hardship and danger, but a miserable loser driven by self-pity into a stupid snow drift far from everyone. Far from Sarai.

What would happen to Sarai?
And the worst is that he missed calling her yesterday morning.
Like he promised.

9 *Back to the Madhouse*

When Hack woke up the howling was gone. He missed it. Would he ever be that lucky again?

He lay safe and warm in the darkness under his blanket of snow, still on his shoulder facing sideways. His parka still shielded his nose and mouth and maintained a warm breathing space around them.

But he couldn't stay here the rest of his life.

The downside of his lightless safety was he had no idea what was going on around him. By now the sun could have come up, but he had no way to know. He waited in darkness for what seemed another three hours. Or was it three minutes? No way to tell. He had read about sensory deprivation chambers in which people lost all measure of time. He was in one.

He remembered times in his bedroom back home he'd risen into winter dark, thinking by now it must be seven or eight in the morning, only to discover from his clock it was not even two.

Back home that mistake was just an irritating inconvenience. He'd go back to bed and hope to return to sleep. He'd read a magazine or watch late night infomercials.

But rising erect into a night time blizzard could cost him his shelter and maybe his life.

On the other hand, this January day was going to be short—at most maybe nine hours' sunlight to get home. He couldn't afford to waste any sunlight and warmth the January day would grant him.

And it was Saturday. He had his regular Saturday night gig at the Madhouse. Hack hadn't missed a performance since he'd moved back to Ojibwa City. Gigs were hard to come by. No shortage of bands. Gus and Mattie and the others counted on him.

Hack understood that in the overall scheme of life and death this was probably a stupid consideration, but he took these obligations seriously.

He did know he had been awake what felt like a long time.

So: Hack started wriggling his torso out of the log. When he managed to get his waist and then his thighs free of their confinement he put his hands on the edge of the log and pushed himself out further. Then he turned and planted his hands on the hard-frozen ground beneath him. He pushed and then rolled and twisted as he propelled himself further until he was all the way out of the log.

Still in total darkness, he lay under the snow for a few moments, waiting for his breathing to slow to something like normal. Then he placed his palms flat on the ground and pushed down in the hardest push-up of his life. When he had lifted his torso about a foot off the ground he pulled his knees in under his belly. He started to rise. He put all his strength into his legs and back to straighten and rise through the weight of snow.

His head popped free into blinding sunlight. He yanked his mittens up through the snow to cover his suddenly burning eyes. He straightened his legs and his back to rise the rest of the way upright. Snow fell off his head and neck. He shook himself like a big two-legged terrier to rid himself of more.

He was still waist deep. He closed his eyes for a moment while he used his mittens to brush off as much as he could every part of his head, shoulders and chest. Then he opened his eyes again.

The glare blinded. He covered his eyes again. Then he lifted one hand enough to peer out through the tiny crack between mitten and forehead. The blizzard had ended. He blinked and waited for his eyes to adjust to the blinding light. Between mitten and cheek he saw a pure blue sky above him and pure white everywhere else.

In the woods boughs hung down from the weight of snow. A few crooked and fallen branches stuck like black scimitars into piles of whiteness.

His feet were still locked in place. He swiveled his torso and looked back over his shoulder towards home: a flat white plain unmarred by any tracks of human or animal. A few low spots dimpled the expanse and an occasional hill bumped up here and there. Occasional black trees dotted the way home. Dead brown leaves hung by black stems.

Otherwise, the lone and level white stretched far away.

A perfect surface for skiing back to town.

A cardinal fluttered down onto a branch about twenty feet away and fifteen high. Hack said, "What are you doing here?" The bird tilted its red head and eyed him as if throwing the same question right back.

"The wolves are gone, so I guess there's just us," Hack said.

The bird took off and disappeared into the woods, as if to let Hack know he was on his own.

Items to take care of before heading home: first, protect his eyes. He unzipped his coat just enough to reach inside with his right hand to feel around for his sunglasses. Through his mitten he felt their shape in his left inside pocket. He had to remove the mitten to snatch the glasses out of his inside left pocket with his bare hand. He stuck the glasses over his nose and jammed his hand back into the mitten.

As often happened, the blizzard carried with it a deep chill. The temperature must have dropped far below zero. In those few seconds, the inside of the mitten already lost its warmth. To keep his thumb warm, he had to nest it inside the larger section of his mitten up against the rest of his hand and the other four fingers. The mitten thumb flapped empty and loose.

Second, the obvious: relieve himself. He made a move to step forward with his right foot, but it was a struggle even to lift his knee. Slowly he pushed his way over a few feet away from his log and made the necessary and scary adjustments to his pants and urinated into the snow and zipped back up as fast as he could.

He returned to his log and probed his night's bed chamber for his skis and found them and pulled them out. He dug some more and felt around for his ski poles and his pack. He dug through his pack for some trail mix and ate the entire packet, washing it down with the remnant of water in the bottle he had socked away inside his coat the previous evening.

To mark the spot of his unique experience, Hack took three empty red, blue and green trail mix packets and tied them into a knot and crammed them into the fork of the highest branch he could reach.

He hoisted his pack onto his back. Then he locked his boots into his skis, hoisted his poles and pointed himself towards home.

Hack's trip back to town was easy. He was strangely well-rested and very satisfied with himself and his survival. He re-established his relaxed rhythm again and felt like he was gliding—the well-earned reward for every sweaty hour he had spent on wheeled training skis through all those weeks of summer heat.

By the time he saw the first scattered houses of town, the sun had dropped low in the sky, which meant it would be after five when he reached his gig. He decided to go around the town directly to the Madhouse.

He approached the Madhouse parking lot from the west. As he herringboned his way through the brush around the pond he saw two squad cars parked close to each other on the far side of the lot. Revolving red lights glowed from their roofs.

The high parking lot light had yet to switch on and only half a moon shown down, so reflections from the massive unplowed snow drifts provided what light there was. Hack spotted the red glow of a cigarette tip. Hack skied directly up to the cigarette glow and angled his skis to a V and to a gentle stop in front of the smoker.

Who wasn't Gus. Mattie jumped back. "Jeez!"

"Sorry, Mattie," Hack said.

She grabbed both hands to her chest. "You should be."

"How's it going?"

"What?"

"How's it going?"

"Not good."

He said, "Sorry to hear that. I just had the most amazing night myself."

"What a thing to say."

Mattie seemed more ticked off than Hack thought she ought to be. But that was Mattie. "I heard the wolves."

"Wolves. And where'd you do that?"

"In the woods, of course. Where the wolves are. Got caught in the blizzard. Thought I was going to die. Kept warm all night in a snow drift. But made it out safe and like I said, amazing."

"That's amazing, all right." She wore a strange expression he couldn't read.

"Where's Gus? He's here for the gig, right?"

"You really don't know, do you?"

"Don't know what?"

"Okay...so first, Gus won't be making the gig."

"Why not?"

"He's under arrest."

"For what?"

"Well, they aren't spelling it out, but a lot of people think it's got something to do with the murder."

He said, "Okay." Then, "there's a murder."

"I'm starting to believe you. You really don't know."

"Which is what I said. But I know Gus didn't murder anyone."

"They're not saying he personally did. They're using words like accomplice or accessory—like that."

"That can't be." Hack turned to ski over to the cop car on the other side of the lot.

As Hack moved by her, Mattie grabbed his left arm near the shoulder of his parka. "Hold it!"

With her left hand she tossed her cigarette into the pond. It sank into the white snow piled on the frozen pond. "I guess in the big picture your ignorance is a good thing. But if I got your story right, it's that you were out in the woods all alone all night, right?"

"Right."

"So you got no alibi."

"Alibi for a murder?"

"It'd help."

"Whose?"

"Amir's."

A vision of Amir's solemn dark face flashed in Hack's mind. His insides chilled colder than they ever had during his night in the wilderness. "Gus had no part in any murder, especially Amir's. Where would they get the idea he's an accomplice?"

"I think they got the idea because his best friend is the killer."

"But I'm his best friend."

"The light dawns. Get it? You. They think you killed Amir. Cops are swarming all over town after you."

"Me. Why me?"

"For starters, the body was found in your basement. And they say he was killed with your knife. There's cops everywhere. Local cops, sheriff's deputies, state cops, and I heard even the F.B.I."

"The F.B.I.?"

"They're calling it an international anti-Muslim hate crime. You're national news. Famous. And our nice little town is famous right along with you."

"I don't hate anybody, least of all Amir. Amir's my friend."

She shook her head. "They talk like it's a sure thing. Like they got all the evidence they need." She pointed at the squad cars. "Can you prove them wrong?"

Hack glanced over at the red lights on the other side of the lot.

"Before you talk to them you better work up a good idea how to prove you didn't do it."

10 Hiding Out

Hack said, "But I haven't done anything."

"Funny. Exactly what Rennie said. He didn't do anything either. And just eighteen months later, free as a bird."

"Maybe that was different."

"Yeah. They only accused him of dealing drugs. They're after you for murder." She paused. "Well, maybe two murders.

"Two? What's the other one?"

"Remember that headless Ahmed guy they found in St. Paul the other day? They're saying you did that one too."

"I never even heard of that guy."

"It's something about the M.O. being the same."

Hack felt like he was sinking into an ever-deepening hole. He stared at Mattie.

Her expression was grim. "So maybe you lay low until you get some idea what's going on. You can always turn yourself in later. If you're sure you're safe."

"Why wouldn't I be safe?"

A car door opened on the far side of the parking lot. A wide burly cop in shiny blue parka emerged from one of the squad cars. The heavy crunch of the man's boots echoed in the cold night air as he ambled in their direction.

Mattie said, "You want to be arrested? Now's your chance."

"What's my other choice?"

"You need a plan. Or time to think of one."

Nothing came. Hack looked at the approaching cop and then back at Mattie and then back at the cop.

Mattie finger-flicked him on the forehead and the sting broke the spell. "Tell you what. Ski over to my house. They haven't had a chance to plow side streets. Keep to the side. Don't be seen—but don't make it obvious you're trying not to be seen. In a few minutes I'll drive home and let you in."

"I could explain to the cops where I was when it happened."

"Can you prove to the cops where you were when it happened?"

Like all the best true stories, Hack's was incredible—a bad thing in an alibi. "Maybe not."

The high parking lot lamp switched on. He and Mattie stood in brilliant white light, their crooked shadows stark on the heaps of snow.

Mattie said, "I know all about cops. They've got two murders to explain. Once they grab you, they'll never want to let you go. If the original excuse doesn't pan out, they'll find another even if they have to invent one. There's a good chance you'll never see the sun again."

Hack stayed rooted to the spot.

Mattie stuck her face up to his. She poked his chest with stiffened fingers. "Move!"

Hack moved. He turned and launched himself out of the parking lot and propelled himself onto the snow and outside the pool of electric light, temporarily safe in relative darkness.

As he skied away, he heard Mattie shouting, "Hey Rolf? Any news?"

The cop shouted something Hack couldn't make out.

Mattie answered. "Just a punk I sent on his way."

One final glance over Hack's shoulder showed Mattie strolling to meet the cop. Hack turned his attention to skiing.

Like she said, the side streets remained unplowed. It took him fewer than twenty minutes to reach Mattie's house. To avoid street lights and passing headlights he herringboned around to her back yard next to her back steps where the shadows seemed deepest.

He took off his skis and ski boots and put on his snow boots. He sat down and leaned his skis and himself against the cold concrete foundation wall.

The pack poked into his back and reminded him he still had it strapped on. He wriggled out of it and laid it over his crossed legs and reached inside. No snacks left. The water bottles were empty.

He started to shiver. He hugged himself but he couldn't stop. Maybe it was the cold finally getting to him now he'd stopped moving.

Maybe it was exhaustion. Maybe it was shock at Amir's murder and his own suddenly precarious situation.

Along with the tremors came a seemingly contradictory detachment. He recognized this absence of feeling. Hack had experienced this shock-into-numbness the day two husky security guards had hustled Hack out of Gogol-Chekhov, his arms cradling his pathetic cardboard box with his few photos and the bedraggled Swedish Ivy in a four-inch flower pot.

He had known other moments like that in his life, but as he sat in the cold darkness it seemed to him the past few years those moments had been crowding closer together` and more frequent, coming at him one after another almost without interruption. Sometimes they seemed to stretch for months—what once had been distinct moods and moments were condensing into a single permanent condition—his life from now on.

He sat shivering for an hour or so and then heard a car engine. In the driveway he saw a glow of auto headlamps lighting the front of Mattie's garage. The expanding yellow-white circles revealed old brown boards under the garage's cracked and peeling white paint.

He recognized Mattie's dark pickup as it pulled forward into the driveway. It stopped with the engine idling. Mattie stepped down from the driver side.

He watched her slender figure as she stepped into the light cast by her headlamps. Mattie was direct and forceful in all her movements. Mattie didn't walk to the garage door; she strode up to it like a linebacker approaching the line of scrimmage. She slammed the door upwards so hard it rattled and echoed around after it reached the top.

Mattie returned to her truck and drove it into the garage. She turned off the engine and got out again and then reached up and slammed down the garage door even harder than she had lifted it. The banging broke Hack's spell. "Hey, Mattie. I'm over here."

"Quiet! You think the cops can't find out we're friends?"

Hack muttered, "I didn't know that myself."

Head down and appearing to fumble in her bag for her keys, she walked past him as if he weren't there. She stepped up to her back door. She unlocked it and flung it open. Without glancing in his direction, she spoke in a low voice. "You got ten seconds to get your ass through this door."

Hack lurched to his feet, hoisted his pack in one arm and scrambled through her door into her kitchen. He collapsed back down on the floor in the corner closest to the basement stairs and leaned against the wall.

Mattie said, "I'll grab your skis."

She disappeared for a moment, then returned hugging his skis and poles to her chest. "Take off your boots. We'll get all your stuff into the basement."

Using the wall for partial support, Hack scooted himself half way up. Hands still shaking, he stripped off his parka and let it drop to the floor. He settled back down onto the floor and bent forward to unlace his boots. The laces were stiff and strange in his fingers and he got no good purchase at all. He felt like a two-year-old.

Mattie knelt down in front of him. "Relax," she said. She removed his hands from the boots. She untied his left boot, then worked it off his foot with seemingly uncharacteristic gentleness. Then she did likewise for his right. She said, "Stay here." She straightened and carried the boots and the ski gear down her basement stairs.

A moment later, she reappeared with some clothes in her arms. "Rennie left some stuff behind. Get up."

Hack tried to stand up straight. He had to lean against the wall again. Even the wall didn't seem enough. Mattie came over and offered her shoulder. He draped his left arm over her shoulder. She supported him as she led him through the living room into her bedroom. He noticed the computer on the small table in the corner. "Hey, you still haven't hooked it up," he said.

She dumped him onto her bed. "Just like you to notice that. Get out of your clothes and into these." She dumped her armful of Rennie's clothing on top of him, then disappeared again.

He lay on his back and stared up at her ceiling and saw faded wallpaper. An eagle fought an owl. Actually, many eagles fought many owls. A pattern. Every raptor spread its wings and extended its talons towards its enemy.

Who puts wallpaper on a ceiling? Or maybe that's normal. Maybe he should pay more attention to ceilings. For all he knew, there could have been wallpaper on all the ceilings of all the rooms he was ever in. Maybe he should be paying more attention to more ceilings more often.

An instant later, he was unconscious.

11 A Night at Mattie's

Hack woke up lying on his back. Light bounced off snow drifts through the unshaded window. He could almost have read by it.

Compared to his night before in the log, he wallowed in luxury. He lay on a bed covered in heavy wool blankets. His head rested on a soft pillow.

On the ceiling above he made out the same owls and eagles still frozen in their eternal battles.

He became aware of the warmth of Mattie's body to his right. He looked over and saw she was facing away on her side. She breathed soft and steady. He went back to sleep.

A ring from his phone jolted him. By habit he checked to his right where the phone at home always sat in its charging cradle. Then he remembered. The phone was ringing from a pocket of his back pack. Mattie must have dumped his pack there on the floor by the bed.

With as much quiet and care as he could muster he slid left out from under his blankets and off the bed. He bent down and lifted his pack off the floor and pawed for the pocket with the jangling phone.

He twisted the pack around and around for the right pocket. The phone rang the full seven times he had set it for. By the time he unzipped the right pocket and got the phone into his bare hand the ringing had stopped.

"Are you thinking at all?" Mattie asked. She was sitting up in bed, her blankets wrapped around her. "Don't you know they can use your phone to track you?"

He read the phone's recent call list. Caller ID was blocked. "I didn't know anyone was going to want to track me."

"Well, turn it off now."

"I did. I thought I had if off."

"Was it the cops?"

"No idea." He clambered back into the bed and yanked the blankets over him. "God, it's cold."

"I know. Too broke to pay for much heat," she said. "Just enough to keep the pipes from freezing."

"Well, my pipes are freezing right now."

She pulled her body up next to him. "We'll bundle for warmth."

He felt the heat of her skin against his shoulder and back. It was nice. Then he realized it was her bare skin—the weight of her soft naked breast on his own naked arm. "How can you sleep naked in this cold?"

"I always sleep naked."

"Oh God."

"I hate bras," she said. "I sure can't stand to sleep in one."

"How about pajamas? Or sweat shirts and sweat pants? Or something."

"Just go back to sleep. You need it."

The silence stretched. He spoke. "The divorce came through."

"Sorry—that's tough for you."

"Yeah."

"Can't wait for mine to come through."

"So you know."

He felt her sit up next to him. From what he could see of her face, there might have been a hint of a smirk.

"Know what?"

"You know."

"No clue."

"Just so you know."

"Whatever, soldier. I think we both need more sleep. Especially you." She lay back down and nestled against him again.

He lay there for a while more. She seemed asleep.

He realized he was happy. Ecstatic even. Which was nuts. Too many emotions too fast. Slow down. Maybe I'm going crazy. But who wouldn't?

He spoke into the darkness. "Why'd you call me 'soldier'?"

She groaned. "Do we need to talk about that now?"

"I'm wondering, that's all."

"For God's sake, get some sleep."

"I'm nothing like a soldier. I've never even been in the military."

"If you've never been in the military, how do you know if you're like a soldier?"

"My dad was a Marine. I knew him pretty well. He was in combat in Vietnam. My grandfather was killed in Europe in World War Two, so of course I never got to meet him at all."

"And you're nothing like them?"

"Not that I know."

"Did you know your dad before he served in Vietnam?"

"I wasn't born yet."

"Then how do you know what he was like before? Anyway, I've known lots of soldiers. Rennie was a soldier—before he became an asshole. He was in Iraq and Afghanistan. And you just seem to me like a soldier."

"In what way?"

She sighed. "In a lot of ways, that's all."

"But you can't be specific?"

"Rennie always said a soldier knows to grab any sleep he can get while he can get it."

"My dad used to say the same thing."

"See?" She pulled herself even closer. He felt the light tickle of her hair across his arm. Eventually he slept.

12 An Ogre For Our Time

Hack woke into bright daylight. Mattie stood by the bed, pulling a red sweatshirt down over her head. "Work," she said.

"What is you do, anyway?"

"I waitress five times a week at Berringer's. Haven't you seen me there? Top spot in town."

"Don't get out much."

"Today's the Sunday morning after-service Church crowd. Mark will need me there. Plus I think it's a good idea to keep doing everything like normal."

"Okay."

"Don't leave the house. Don't make any phone calls. Don't turn that frigging phone back on."

She stepped over and pulled down the shade on the window. "Stay away from any unshaded windows. When you get hungry, you'll find some things in the fridge. I already made coffee. I'll bring some food when I come back. But not too much, I guess. Got to act like I'm still cooking for one."

"Thanks."

"You're welcome."

"I mean, thanks for taking charge."

"I know you didn't kill that guy."

"How?"

"I've been watching you twenty years, especially lately. It's not in you."

"Thanks for that too."

She bent down and placed her warm fingers on Hack's forehead. "No fever, that's good. I'll scope the situation. Maybe I'm wrong and you should turn yourself in." She straightened up. "See you soon"—she smiled—"Soldier."

Hack watched her out the bedroom door, then heard her open and slam the back door. A moment later her he heard her truck start up and back out the drive way and zoom off.

He slept again.

When Hack finally pushed himself out of bed, it was after eleven. He was still dressed in Rennie's clothes. They were too big. He had to roll up the pants legs and the shirt sleeves. The cold floor stung his feet. He found his wool socks in the bathroom, hanging to dry along with the rest of his clothes. Only the socks were dry enough to wear. He put those on and walked into the kitchen.

He saw through the kitchen window that Mattie had left the garage door up. Nothing to be done—he shouldn't show himself outside the house.

Anyway, maybe she left it up on purpose? Maybe one more signal to the world she was the only one home? Maybe she's pretty smart?

But is she smart enough for the both of us?

And why is there a "both of us" in the first place? How did that happen—if it did? One more mystery in a life that was turning into a streak of terrible mysteries smacking him one after the other. He should count himself lucky there was one nice mystery mixed in with all the crappy ones.

He poured himself a cup of coffee from the pot, then turned off the heating plate. The coffee had been sitting there for hours, so it was bitter. The bitterness helped wake him.

He felt no hunger at all, but he did suffer a huge thirst. He found a white plastic twelve-ounce souvenir Twins cup in a pantry. He filled it with cold water at the sink and drank it down in one gulp. Then he filled and gulped it down twice more. The cold burn of near-ice water on his throat woke him more.

He wandered out to the living room and turned on the TV. No reception. In fact, no cable box. He supposed that had been one more luxury lost in the impoverishment from Mattie's divorce.

And since there were no local stations in the Ojibwa City near-wilderness, there was no TV reception at all.

He returned to her bedroom and sat down at the table and in a few minutes made the necessary attachments to get the computer he'd given her up and running.

He searched the "available networks" list. Mattie had no home network, but there was an unsecured network available. It belonged to what must be a nearby coffee house: "Sven's Hot Mug." He connected to Sven's network.

The first thing he did was log into his email provider's server to check his email.

Thousands of emails clogged his Inbox. The only friendly ones were the spam. The others blazed:

"You die, Racist!"

"Racist Islamophobic killer."

"I HATE YOU BECAUSE YOU HATE! HATE!"

"White supremacy is the root of all evil."

"I hope they catch you and string you up!"

Didn't these people have jobs?

The rage didn't shock him. This wasn't Hack's first experience with unreasoning hatred. In fact, the emails seemed to Hack the next logical step after Gogol-Chekhov.

But how'd they all know his email address? Had someone doxed him?

His next foray was to the ZNN site. It was ZNN who had exposed his identity by revealing his full name, his home address, his phone number, and his email address. He wondered why they hadn't posted his social security number and DNA profile.

Hack had leapt with no middle phase from total obscurity to international infamy. According to ZNN, the F.B.I. had fingered him as a "person of interest" in the grisly murder of small town business man Amir Mohammed as well as a St. Paul man named Ahmed Abadi.

Hack ran across a videoed news conference run by the F.B.I. agent in charge of the investigation. A tall gaunt man in a dark suit and nearly phosphorescent white shirt stood without overcoat at a microphone outdoors somewhere. A squad of heavy set grim-faced officials in overcoats and parkas flanked him. High piles of snow framed the shot, so it was probably Minnesota. "For a variety of reasons, we need to interview Wilder as soon as possible."

Someone shouted from behind the camera. "Agent Blanding, you say 'person of interest.' Is it more accurate to call Wilder a suspect?"

"We very much want to talk to Mr. Wilder."

"Do you have any idea where he is?"

"If we did, we would have talked with him by now."

"So you don't know where he is?"

One of his fellow officials stepped up from behind and muttered something.

"We do have some information that Mr. Wilder has fled the area. Regardless, if he sees this, we heartily recommend to Mr. Wilder that he turn himself in."

The same official stepped up and muttered something again.

Agent Blanding said, "Please make the public aware there is a reward of $50,000 offered by the Council on Muslim American Relations."

"What can you say about the evidence against him?"

"We can say we very much want to talk with him."

The officials and reporters kept looping through more of the same. Hack abandoned that video and found another clip from ZNN.

It is some kind of panel discussion. A spectrally thin older woman frowned into the camera. "We've asked legal affairs correspondent Lauren Goodwell to examine the suspect's background. Lauren, what have you learned so far about this Nathanael Andrew Wilder?"

Hack noticed she used all three names—like Lee Harvey Oswald or John Wayne Gacy. Bad sign.

The camera panned back to reveal two others sitting with the woman behind some kind of semicircular desk with a rounded front. There was a younger woman with a swept back hairdo and a pink scarf and an even younger black guy with glasses and a bright red bow tie.

The younger woman—apparently Lauren: "We've learned a lot,

Jane. Since Gogol-Chekhov fired him, Nathanael Andrew Wilder has blazed a trail of hate speech and white supremacist ideology. The company won't publicly say why they fired him, but inside sources tell us they had no choice. He was notorious for creating what they termed a hostile work environment."

Jane: "Isn't that the term courts use for expressions of hate?"

Lauren: "Exactly, Jane. We don't know the details, but for Gogol-Chekhov to have fired him cold would certainly have required displays of animus incurable by normal means such as bias training. And as many university studies have established, animus like that always extends to Muslims."

Lauren continued: "The bitterness from his termination apparently turned him into a loner. After his wife divorced him, he moved back from St. Paul to his original tiny home town of Ojibwa City to run some kind of marginal one-person computer repair business. He subsequently lost custody of his child, which given his psychology could only have made matters worse."

Hack found himself muttering at the screen: "That's not true. They court gave us joint custody of Sarai."

Lauren: "So here is our very volatile scenario. A bitter impoverished loner loses all connection to the rest of society. He stews over his hopeless personal situation and craves someone to blame. Islamophobia and other forms of white supremacist ideology fester until he finally finds and fixates on an innocent target for his rage."

Jane: "What have you learned about the specific evidence against him?"

Lauren: "The evidence against Wilder is certainly compelling. Police found the victim's body in Wilder's basement. There's no doubt the murder weapon belonged to him. It's a particularly savage kind of military knife used for up close work by Marines and Special Forces. Here's a photo of the type of knife we're talking about."

(On the screen a file photo of a Kabar knife.)

Lauren (continuing in narration): "Notice the jagged serrations near the handle. Very brutal, and consistent with the wounds on Mr. Mohammed. Investigators won't say publicly, but we have sources who tell us the victim's head was completely severed."

Jane: "Do we know what specific incident incited Wilder to such savagery?"

Lauren back on camera: "The military nature of the weapon reveals a man clinging to militaristic fantasies. For obvious reasons, the F.B.I. won't tell us all their investigation has uncovered so far, but forensic psychiatrist and former F.B.I. profiler Dr. Somerset Malmo shared some thoughts with me about the kind of alienated white man who ventures into murderous fantasies which explode into murderous violence. Suffice to say, Wilder is certainly a bitter and angry man."

Jane: "We'll have that interview with Dr. Malmo in our next segment."

Lauren: "We did find an alt-right website with postings by a "Nathaniel Wilder." They were full of anti-Muslim rants we won't repeat here."

(On the screen a page filled with obscene words in giant capital letters punctuated with random exclamation points and bearing the name Nathaniel Wilder emblazoned on it.)

Hack: "That's not me. That's Nathaniel. I'm Nathanael. With an 'a.' Whoever he is, he doesn't even spell his name the same."

(Bow Tie on Screen): "It just keeps happening doesn't it? They come out of the wood work—or small town American woods in this case—simmering with fear and hatred against non-white peoples and then they vent their frustrations on the nearest dark skinned victim."

Jane, shaking her head in sadness: "That is so true, Tad. There is so much ignorance, bigotry and hatred harbored in rural dark places. The country is changing. Those fearful of change cling to the past and strike out blindly at anyone whose skin is a different shade or speaks with an accent or most frightening of all worships differently."

Jane (continuing): "Lauren, do investigators have any idea what there was specifically about Mr. Mohammed in particular that excited so much raw rage from Wilder?"

Lauren: "We know Mr. Mohammed was a refugee from Iraq. That's all they'll tell us. There may be some national security implication, which may partly explain federal involvement. Authorities are refusing to tell us why Mohammed left Iraq or how he wound up in an out-of-the way location like Ojibwa City."

Lauren (continuing): "Or a simple business dispute may have triggered a rage killing. We know Wilder did some work on Mr. Mohammed's computer. Maybe there was a dispute over payment."

Todd: "What about his alleged accomplice?"

Lauren: "Authorities are tight-lipped about this man Augustus Albert Dropo. They have him in custody. They won't say anything about the evidence they have against him, but it must be quite substantial."

Jane: "Dropo already has obtained a very well-known attorney. Here he is."

Gus's lawyer was indeed well-known. It was Lily's father Sam Lapidos.

(Clip of Sam Lapidos): "My client is just as repulsed as anyone else by this horrific crime. In fact, Mr. Mohammed was a man he knew, respected and liked. My client is not guilty of this crime and we will fight this baseless and outrageous prosecution every step of the way." (End clip).

Lauren: "The usual boilerplate, no?"

Jane (shaking her head in sadness, then): "Tad, how is the local community reacting?"

Tad: "Jane, I was out to Minnesota yesterday and I interviewed many local leaders. The general response from the local folk has frankly been disappointing, but it's heartening to see there is a minority in the community responding with some degree of appropriate outrage. We find some hope in the presence of a minority that doesn't want their community to be associated with this crime. In fact, they're putting on a special event to dramatize their rejection of hatred. Here's community activist Tariq Daghestani."

(Tariq Daghestani on screen.): "We're asking the entire

community to join us this Wednesday night at the MinneCentre in St. Paul for a very special event we're calling "Rock The Unity."

"Rock The Unity will be an opportunity for all of us to make a bold and courageous statement about who we are and who we are not. We will affirm and celebrate one another with food and art and music from many cultures. The world-famous singer Fredra Kolo has already agreed to perform. We invite everyone from all faiths, Christian, Jewish, Muslim and of course people of indigenous religion, along with those who profess no particular faith at all. We will all come together to reject hatred and celebrate unity and will gather as one Minnesota family—a true family affair."

Hack took Daghestani at his word—"Rock The Unity" would indeed be a family affair—Hack's family. First he'd seen his former father-in-law Sam Lapidos. Now, a little behind Daghestani and to his left, her face somber and sad, stood Lily.

13 Feds On The Job

A little after two P.M., Hack heard Mattie's car pull up the driveway.

Hack had given up on the news and its drumbeat of slander towards him. He lay on the living room couch with his phone in his lap, where it had sat for an hour. By great force of will he had resisted turning it on. He was desperate to talk to the one person in the world whose love was unconditional—partly to explain, but mostly just to hear her voice.

He heard Mattie slam down the garage door and stomp through the back door of the house. The refrigerator door opened and closed. A moment later she trailed snow into the living room gripping an open bottle of beer in her left hand. She flopped back down on a big stuffed chair and chugged a third of the bottle and wiped her cheek with the back of her hand. She stared up at the ceiling. "God I'm beat."

"I'm sorry about the whole thing. I didn't mean to put you through this."

She shot him a hard glare. "My choice."

A moment later, she said, "Sorry—tough day."

"No problem."

"Did you get more sleep?"

"I slept fine. Then I had nothing else to do, so I set up your computer and Internet and watched the news. It seems I'm the biggest fiend out there."

"You'll do till the next fiend comes along," she said. "I had a sort of scare myself. With the feds."

"What feds?"

"F.B.I. agents stormed the café. Scared the crap out of me. For a second I thought they came because they knew about you being here."

"I guess they didn't."

"Right. Not yet. I think they came that way to intimidate. Turned out they were just questioning people."

"About what?"

"About you, Soldier. Who you hang out with. Any crackpot groups you belong to. Do you you put milk or cream on your cereal? Whether you snore. Do you pay your taxes? Who'd you beat up in grade school? Whether you spend a lot more money than you look like you should have. Ever show signs of incipient anti-social behavior? What groups do you hate? What are your favorite drugs? What music do you like? Whether you talk a lot about politics or religion or sex."

"What'd you tell them?"

"Nothing. In fact, nobody told them squat. You'd have thought nobody knew your name. I was proud. After a while the feds got these pissed off faces and took off. I don't think they're having any luck anywhere in this town."

One more thing Hack hadn't anticipated. "I'm amazed."

Mattie said, "Somehow you've earned a lot of friends in this town. Or maybe no one trusts the feds."

"Didn't Amir have friends?"

"Sure. But nobody thinks you beheaded him, for God's sake."

"You included?"

"Short answer—no."

"Great. But…"

"But?"

"But I was sitting here and I got to thinking. I feel sort of bad about the way I talked to you last night."

"What way?"

"When we were in bed together. You know."

"No I don't."

"It was probably the exhaustion talking. I hope I didn't make you uncomfortable."

She peered at him. "Uncomfortable."

"Yeah."

"When I'm uncomfortable, I'll let you know."

"I hope it's never necessary, but if it is I'll welcome your doing that."

"You're serious, aren't you?" She stood up for an instant and immediately sat back down and folded her arms over her chest. She shook her head and sighed a big showy sigh that turned into a moan. "Who did this to you? And why'd you let them?"

"Sorry."

"Every wrong word isn't an insult. Every tiny thing doesn't offend. Every less-than-perfect moment isn't a catastrophe. Get it?"

"I guess."

"You guess."

Time to find another subject. He said, "You know, sooner or later they're going to find out about you and me working together in the band. They'll wonder if you know something about where I am."

"Probably sooner."

"I can't stay here."

"You got somewhere else to go?"

"Maybe."

She nodded. "Good. Don't tell me where."

"I won't."

"Smart for once." She glanced down at the phone by him on the couch. "You didn't turn on that phone, did you?"

"No. Much as I want to."

"Who you got so important to call?"

"Sarai. My daughter. She's nine."

"Oh." Mattie stood and went into her bedroom. She returned a moment later with a brown leather bag zipped on top. It was a bit smaller then the average airline carry-on. She set it down on the floor and unzipped the top and began to lay out its contents. "This might help."

As Mattie unloaded the bag's goodies onto the floor, Hack poked through the pile: a foil blanket; three empty water bottles; a first aid kit; a change of thin light pants, shirt and socks; two flashlights; a packet of water purification tablets; a roll of hundred-dollar bills in a metal clip; a Swiss Army knife; a six-inch hunting knife, a little red butane lighter; gloves; a set of burglar tools; a pack of wet wipes; several phone chargers; some items he didn't immediately recognize; and a pile of small black cell phones. The kicker was the two inch-long bars of gold authenticated by the stamp of the Canadian Mint. "What is this stuff?"

"Gus handed me this bag last summer. 'In case'."

"Why would he do that?" Hack recalled that Gus had given him a somewhat larger green metal box with a similar phrase. Without ever peeking inside, Hack had buried it in a hole by his foundation, just outside his house. The feds probably had their hands on it by now. But maybe not?

She shrugged. "You know Gus. He likes to cover all the possibilities. He called it a 'go bag'—in case he develops a sudden need to go—like you got right now."

"A Gus Go Bag with no gun?"

"Any guns we had, Rennie took. Gus would have predicted that too."

Hack picked up one of the phones, a Korean model. "Do these have service?"

"He told me they're all set up. Burners with prepaid long-term contracts. I'm sure Gus would want you to have all this."

"He's not dead, you know."

"You know what I mean."

"You think it's safe to call Sarai on one of these?"

"Gus is pretty sharp on things like that."

"Even if I call from here in the house."

She laid a gentle hand on his shoulder and looked him in the eye. "That's a chance I'll take. Your daughter will have heard things by now. She'll be terrified. Call her."

Hack took a phone into the bedroom. He poked at its few buttons until he found the right one and held it down. The phone came on. The battery measured only 60%, but the phone was working.

Lily had wanted Sarai to have her own cell phone—"for emergencies, if nothing else"—and the time he called the idea ridiculous—"a seven-year-old with her own phone?"

After the separation, it was an argument he was glad he'd lost. He called Sarai directly nearly every day or evening to check in with her. And he didn't have to go through Lily.

He dialed Sarai's phone. It rang several times. Then he heard her voice. A tentative "Hello?"

Hack's throat constricted. He could barely choke out her name. "Sarai."

"Dad?" she whispered. "Is that you?"

"Yes."

"Mom's been crying the whole day."

"I'm sorry, Sweetie."

"Don't come here."

"I won't—not just yet."

"You're in big trouble, aren't you?"

"Some."

"Don't talk down to me, Dad. I know better. And I heard something else."

"What's that?"

"I heard Uncle Amir is dead. It's true, right?"

"It is true, Sarai. I'm sorry."

Her little girl voice turned to a whisper. "I know you didn't hurt him. They're just lying."

"Of course."

"You better get off the phone, Dad. I saw on a detective show they can track these things. What if they're bugging my phone?"

"I just wanted to make sure you're okay. And so you know, wherever I am I'll call every day just like normal."

"It's not normal, Dad. Now get off the line."

He heard a voice—Lily's he thought—"Who's that, Sarai?"

"It's Brett, Mom. From school." Then she said, "Gotta go, Brett. Talk to you tomorrow." The click told Hack she'd ended the call.

Hack held the button down to turn off his phone. An impulse seized him and he threw it against the wall. The loud thwack startled him. He'd not made so much as a single violent gesture towards anyone or anything for years. A moment later, Mattie appeared in the doorway.

"Sorry," he said. "Bad moment. But Sarai's okay, anyway. Considering."

Mattie grinned and picked the phone off the floor. "Probably good for you." She turned serious. "But don't use that phone again," she said. "That's why Gus put a bunch in the bag."

"I won't."

"In fact, I'll pull a Hillary and smash it and toss it in a dump later. By the way, I don't see any food gone. Did you eat anything at all today?"

"Never thought of it."

"So you are hungry, right?"

The pain stabbed his belly. "Now that you mention it."

"Come in the kitchen. I'll have something in a few minutes."

Once again his legs weighed heavy. He shuffled into the kitchen and seated himself with care at the kitchen table.

Mattie followed him in and passed by to the freezer. "Nothing fancy this time," she said. "Just a frozen pizza."

Twenty minutes later he was burning his mouth on melted cheese.

She opened a bottle of beer and set it on the table. "This may help. But slow down."

He didn't.

She watched him for a moment. "I guess that pizza's yours," she said. "I'll make another one."

After he let her help finish the second pizza, he went to the refrigerator and took a second beer and opened it with the bottle opener nailed to the wall.

The refrigerator door sported the usual magnets and notes with funny captions. A few magnets pinned photos on the door. There was a photo of Mattie with an older woman who looked like her and was probably her mother, another photo of her and a man Hack didn't know, his face X'd out—Rennie?—and another of Mattie with a small round boy, both of them smiling into the camera.

Hack said, "That's Little Gus, isn't it?"

"A few years ago."

"I never connected you with Little Gus. But of course you'd know him."

"Of course," she said. "He's a sweet kid."

"I suppose it's stupid of me not to make the connection."

"I suppose," she agreed. "He had some problems after his mother left and I kind of helped out."

"Is that a thing with you—helping out males in trouble?"

"Only baby males."

"You're helping me out."

"Proves my point."

"You know, you're nothing like I thought."

"Yes I am. I'm exactly like you thought. It's just that sometimes I'm nothing like I thought."

It crossed Hack's mind that Mattie might have said something revealing and profound, but deep exhaustion slowed his mind to a crawl and he couldn't follow the thought through. "Do you mind if I nap?

14 Hack & Mattie in the night

Once again Hack woke in the dead of night. This time he knew
instantly where he was—in Mattie's bed. He was lying on his back under
the same heavy blankets. He felt her warm naked body against his. He
turned his head. Her head lay on his shoulder. Her breathing was even
and quiet. Somehow sensing his glance, she opened her eyes. He
surprised himself by kissing her on the nose. She smiled and closed her
eyes again.

Sometime later, he woke again. This time, she was awake first.

He asked, "Why are you grinning like that?"

"I'm sorry if I'm making you uncomfortable."

"There's no way I'm going to live that down, is there?"

"No."

He kissed her on the lips and she kissed him back. They fell
asleep intertwined in the warmth of sheets and heavy blankets and naked
bodies.

At some later moment, with no recollection precisely how or
when it had begun, Hack woke again, this time to the realization they
were making love. He was inside her. Her arms were grasped together
behind his neck. Her eyes were closed and she was moaning. She
answered him powerful thrust for thrust. Neither spoke.

After they finished they lay together awhile and didn't speak and
caressed some more and fell asleep again.

At dawn the shattering wail of police sirens and the noise of
slamming car doors penetrated the walls and jolted Hack awake. He
jumped out of bed and lurched to the window.

Squad cars seemed to be everywhere. An instant later, he felt
Mattie grabbing his upper arm. They stared out together.

Hack fought the acid panic rising in his throat. No way he'd
escape. But what about Mattie? The cops would arrest her too. He'd say
he forced himself into her house. No way Mattie should suffer for his
sake.

But as moments passed, he saw he'd been wrong. It wasn't what he'd thought at first. Mattie's house was not the target.

Mattie's house stood on the corner. Across the side street and a few doors down stood a small red brick building. There was a big candy-striped canopy behind it, the kind under which management could spread summer tables and chairs. But instead of tables Hack counted three squad cars. Five more cars spread out over the yard and on the street in front of the building. Roof lights spun red in every direction. All the cars had their doors flung open. Uniformed cops crouched behind the open doors with drawn pistols and shot guns pointed at the building. Sprinkled among the cops were plain clothes types in blue parkas with the raised yellow letters "F.B.I." on their backs.

A team of uniformed cops rushed the building's door with a ram and battered it in.

"What is that place?" Hack asked.

"It's Sven's Hot Mug," Mattie said. "A local coffee house."

"Uh oh."

"What do you mean?" She tugged at his arm. "Let's get away from the window."

As Hack stepped away, his foot caught on a sheet and he almost tripped. He righted himself. Blankets and sheets were strewn all over the bed and all around the floor. "I guess we were in a hurry."

Mattie tugged his arm again. "What did you mean, 'Uh oh'?"

"When I got on the Internet yesterday, I logged into Sven's free customer network. It was close enough to your house. The feds must have some way of figuring out that was me."

"How?"

"I bet it was when I logged into the server to check my email." He shook his head. "I'm really rotten at this fugitive thing."

"Uh oh."

"Which means that after they don't find me at Sven's they're going to wonder if I'm at least someplace nearby."

"What comes next after 'uh oh'?"

"I clear out."

They stared at each other an instant.

In the heat or cold of the moment, they'd both jumped out of bed naked. Hack sprinted barefoot into the bathroom where he found his own clothes still hanging. He felt them—now dry. He began yanking on his underwear and his socks and kept dressing until he was fully clothed.

Mattie stood at the bathroom door dressed in sweat pants and a sweat shirt. She was holding his coat and boots in her arms. "Don't tell me where you're going."

"I won't."

"And don't forget the Gus Go Bag."

"I won't."

"And don't forget me."

"I can't." He went over to kiss her. He felt the wet on his cheek. He pulled away and saw there were tears in her eyes. "Please don't cry," he said.

"I'm not. Why are you?"

"I'm not either," he lied.

15 Hack's First Plan

Hack came up with a plan. He knew it wasn't much, but he gave himself a pass because after all it was his first.

Mattie and he would wait and hope for the cops to disperse from the neighborhood after they failed to find him at Sven's. Mattie could load his skis and poles in the truck bed. Hack would duck down low on the passenger side of Mattie's truck while she drove him out to the parking lot at the Madhouse. The Madhouse was closed Monday mornings and with reasonable luck no one would be around. From the parking lot, Hack could ski to his next hiding place, which he didn't tell her.

"Decent, but you missed two things," Mattie said.

"What's that?"

"Remember what your dad said? Eat while you can, Soldier. And take a shower, please. In fact, start with the shower."

Hack showered, dressed again in his stale but dry outfit and then stuffed everything from the Gus Go Bag into his back pack.

He made coffee and she heated another pizza. Neither spoke while they prepared the meal nor afterwards while they shared it.

Mattie slipped outside to scout and returned and reported that the cops were no longer visible.

Mattie strolled out to the garage and lifted the garage door. She kept her head up, to all appearances indifferent to any possible onlookers. She gently laid his skis and poles and back pack onto the truck bed.

She backed the truck halfway down the driveway and stopped. He scooted out her back door and into the passenger side. Once they were clear of the driveway and headed down the street he ducked down into the small space in the cab behind the driver's seat.

They maintained their silence for most of the trip. At one point, he muttered from behind her, "Take it easy, please. I don't want to draw attention."

"This is the way I drive," she said. "Rolf and the other cops all know me. If I drive any other way, that'll draw attention."

After a few minutes she pulled into the Madhouse parking lot and stopped. "This is it." She faced straight forward.

He peeked out. The building was dark. No one in the vicinity. He clambered out and retrieved his skis and poles and back pack.

He pulled down his ski mask and pulled the parka hood over his head. He came up to the driver door. "This is it," he said.

She still faced forward. "Don't get caught—at least not 'til you got something to say to talk your way out of this."

"I won't."

"And for sure don't get killed."

"Why would I do that?"

She turned her head and looked at him. "Because you don't know what you're doing."

Her eyes still on him she gunned the engine and the truck lurched forward. Her rear wheels showered debris all over Hack as he stood there. A few shards of ice spattered against his ski mask. She careened onto the road and away.

Hack bent down and put on his skis and hoisted on his pack and set off.

16 Home Again

Compared to Hack's most recent ski jaunt, this one was a snap. Though the day was cold, the sun shone bright in a cloudless blue sky. He carried a pack full of supplies that now incorporated extra gear from Gus. He was in decent physical condition and well fed and considering everything reasonably well rested.

Like the good soldier Mattie seemed to think he could be, Hack tried to make good use of his time on the snow. He wanted to figure out what was going on. He needed to think clearly. Most of all, he needed a plan.

But emotion interfered. And that hadn't happened in a long time. He had always been a logical thinker. Hadn't he? Just a week or two previous, hadn't he been calm and low-key? On an even keel?

Or as Gus claimed, had he just been inert? In a low-down funk because life wasn't going his way? A kind of human robot—what did they call those, androids?—going through the mechanical motions of life, but feeling nothing in particular?

Some distant time in the past, he'd wanted things. He'd worked to get them. Some of them he'd gotten and some he hadn't.

Sometime since he'd lapsed into a mere side line observer. And not an astute observer at that, or right now he'd have a better idea what was going on.

He'd done one thing right. He kept himself fit. He skied around town on his training wheels all summer and fall. When Gus asked why, he explained "Keeping in shape."

"For what?"

To which Hack had no ready answer at the time.

Even his music making was sub-par. He covered other people's songs. The songs were fine but on the other hand he didn't really care about them the way he'd cared back when he was writing his own. His once-a-week band was just a mild diversion to keep his mind off his other mild diversions like writing unmarketable software and playing mediocre chess.

This morning with Mattie he had caught himself crying. Though he did a piss-poor job of hiding it from her. He hadn't cried when GC canned him. He hadn't cried when Lily dumped him. He hadn't cried even when someone hacked his friend Amir to pieces. Hack could make a long list of hurricane-sized tempests through which he had sailed dry eyed.

And the ridiculous tears flowed out of him not three hours after he found himself in near ecstasy. He couldn't remember the last time he had been as happy as he had been for one night sleeping next to Mattie.

And that was before the sex.

Has one woman heating up one pizza turned me into some kind of pussy?

A lot was happening and he understood very little and he understood Mattie least of all.

Even in winter, Hack knew the local tracks and paths well. He just had to keep his eyes open for the telltale red, green and blue wrappers he'd hung high in the fork of the tree branches. In the monochrome world he traveled, the colorful wrappers should jump out like beacons.

After a few misses going back and forth over nearly identical terrain, he spotted the colors. Because of his angle of approach he'd missed them the first two passes.

Close by the tree and its wrappers he found the same rocks, brush and log.

It was almost sundown. He sat down on his log and took a new burner phone out of his pack and dialed Sarai. She answered on the first ring.

"Dad?"

"How'd you know?"

"I don't get other calls from strange numbers."

"Okay to talk?"

"Yes, but please keep it short."

"Short and normal. I insist on my two minutes of normal. Tell me what's going on."

"Seriously?"

"Let's pretend."

"You're not the one's supposed to pretend. That's my job."

"Humor me."

She sighed. "Well, school started up again."

"Anything happening special in school?"

"Really?"

"Yeah, really."

"Well, Tu BiShvat's coming."

"What's that?"

"Don't you remember from last year? It's a holiday. Like a Jewish Arbor Day. It's about planting trees and things. There'll be a party."

"When's that?"

"Thursday night at the JCC. But you can't come."

"You sure?"

"Don't joke."

"Okay."

"Are you going to get out of this fix you're in?"

"Yes."

"Promise?"

"Promise."

"This was already too long. Bye." She clicked off.

"Too short, you mean," Hack muttered and turned off the phone. He found a stone a few inches square embedded in the earth and laid the phone on it. He found a slightly larger stone and smashed the phone and its components.

He couldn't risk a fire. As before, he bedded down for the night inside his log. But the micro-thin insulated blankets out of the Gus Go Bag would keep him toasty.

He hoped to hear the wolves again. Like a kid he tried to stay awake for them, but also like a kid exhaustion and the full nighttime darkness and the cozy warmth shut down his mind and his body and he drifted off.

Hack woke up to the same howling he'd heard before. If wolves were howling it must be night. He lay snug in the darkness enjoying the concert for a while.

Comes a new sound: a patter of feet. Then nearer. Was Sarai right? Did he give the cops his location with the call?

No, the patter's too light and too careful and too quiet for any human being. Animals. Two animals.

The distant howling continues, but now it is accompaniment to a nearer and even more primal vocal.

Two wolves have left their choir mates behind for their own private duet—their own dance and song, the same dance and song every small-town kid grows up recognizing by sight or sound, a mini-fugue of yips and whines to go with the nuzzling and bumping and mounting.

One demanding bark, then more whining, and a series of insistent barks, followed by a quiet moment and then insistent rhythmic thumping.

Hack locks himself in stillness. He breathes slow and shallow as he can. Is what moves him the rational fear of discovery by a pair of dangerous predators or a sincere respect for their privacy?

Well, that's how it's done. That's how Lily and I made Sarai.

After a while the nearby wolves finish and patter off and the faraway wolves stop their howling and Hack fades off to sleep.

17 Hack's Shack

Again Hack woke snug and safe from the cold. No blizzard, no problem. He sidled his now familiar way out of the log and stood up. A bright perfect morning under a bright blue sky. And he had a good idea where to go next. Maybe from there he could finally start accomplishing something positive.

In slightly fewer than four hours' easy traveling, Hack reached a tiny shack on the edge of the woods, perched among trees on the border of a plot of land the Dropo family had owned for generations. The seven-by-ten-foot shack was rickety and unpainted and without electricity, but it was shelter.

And it was obscure. Only a few knew or cared about it. It was far too insignificant to make it onto any official map Hack had ever seen—although Hack had to consider the possibility that these days it might show up in satellite photos.

Back in high school, Gus and Hack had built it together, using a few sheets of plywood and tar paper and various scraps salvaged from an even older shack.

Hack and Gus made a pact never to bring anyone else there, not even girls. It was a private place for the two teenage boys to hide while they snuck their first beers and smokes.

Once Hack moved back to Ojibwa City, it became a private place for the two adult men to hide and drink and smoke. Their only upgrade was a small propane stove.

Hack pulled up to the shack and removed his skis. There were no prints in the snow around it, so no one had visited, at least since the blizzard.

The door hung down from two rusty hinges only four feet off the ground. The door handle was a short piece of rope. Hack unhooked his boots from his skis and pulled the rope up and ducked into the shack, carrying his skis and poles under his left arm. His backpack brushed the top of the door opening. He slung his pack down onto the cracked plywood floor, took out his hiking boots and swapped them for the ski boots. Those he laid on the floor.

He fired up the propane stove and unfolded one of the two wooden slat folding chairs and sat. In a few minutes, the tiny space heated and he took off his ski mask and parka. He leaned back and stretched his feet to warm near the stove.

What now?

This time he was going to shove aside all emotion. This time he'd be logical. He was supposed to be good at that. Although computers mimic intelligence, computers are actually just mindless devices to execute logical instructions in logical sequence. He wrote those instructions. By that logic, logic was his business.

What if any logical connections could there be among all these recent events?

Hack took a small notebook and a pen from his pack and started listed some recent events:

1) Lily divorces me.
2) Someone murders Amir.
3) I'm the chief suspect.
4) I can't prove where I was when it happened.
5) My band misses its gig.
6) I run and hide.
7) For no obvious reason Mattie suddenly likes me.

Not much there. No logical connections at all, except maybe between his divorce and his surprising new relationship with Mattie.

Hack could see the heat waves rising from the stove into the air. He turned down the stove and removed his flannel shirt, now down just to his tee shirt over his thermal.

Broaden the terms. Bring in more events. Hack interrogated himself like he'd seen cops interrogating witnesses on TV: okay, so what else different has happened lately, even if it didn't seem important at the time or didn't seem connected to anything else?

Hack tore out his first page and threw it in the stove and wrote a new list:

1) I find the "Khaybar" text on a discarded computer.

2) I show it to Amir.

3) Amir says he'll check it out.

Logic means I have to distinguish connected from unconnected. So strike the divorce from the list and focus only on events connected to the person who'd been murdered—Amir.

Hack tore out another page and started again:

1) I find the weird "Khaybar" letter on a discarded computer.

2) I show it to Amir.

3) Amir tells me he'll check into it.

4) Amir is murdered with a knife.

5) The killer uses my knife and kills him in my basement.

6) I get blamed.

7) The computer on which I found the "Khaybar" text was also in that same basement where Amir was murdered.

Was the Khaybar computer still there in Hack's basement? Was there a way Hack could find out? None came to mind immediately.

Even in the fierce heat of the shack, Hack felt a sudden chill. There had been at least one other unusual event with an obvious connection. The good dancer. Amalki. Amalki who had been asking about Hack. Amalki whose first impulse when challenged was to brandish a big deadly knife. Amalki who had telephoned Hack and knew where he lived.

Despite his blundering, Hack realized he'd done one thing right. Like a good professional software developer, he always backed things up. Always. The iron rule. For that reason and with some small hope he might get some chance some time to show it to some expert, Hack had copied the Khaybar letter along with every other document from that now lost basement computer onto a flash drive.

He fingered the flash drive in his pants pocket. Still there. Although he could not at that moment imagine what good it would do him.

It was Tuesday morning, a new day, and he hadn't called Sarai.

He took another phone from his pack and turned it on. He had service. He dialed Sarai.

"Dad, I'm supposed to be in school."

"Are you?"

"No, but I'm supposed to be and you shouldn't call me in school."

"Can't help it. I need to hear your voice."

"I've been thinking," she said.

"Good."

"What about Zarah?"

"Zarah?"

"You know. Amir's daughter. My maybe sort-of cousin."

"What about her?"

"Do you think she knows her dad's dead?"

"Sarai, we don't even know Zarah exists."

"She exists. And somebody should tell her. And help her."

"Sarai, even if Zarah exists and even if she's in trouble and even if we could find her, how would we help her?"

"I don't know. I'll think about it. You're busy, so I'll work on it myself and we can talk about it when you take care of all this other stuff."

"Good plan."

"This call is long enough. Bye." Sarai clicked off.

"When you take care of all this other stuff." A daughter's faith in her father's powers.

He heard a noise outside. He turned off the phone and tried to quiet his breathing. Should he turn off the stove? Too late. How long had someone or something been making that noise out there without him noticing?

Each stroke came a few seconds after the previous, a regular repeating soft buzz like a drummer's gentle brushes on a cymbal. The buzz turned louder and became a crunching noise he recognized: boots in the snow. Approaching his shack.

The boot sounds stopped. Then someone was tugging on the rope to open the door.

Hack leapt up, folded the wood chair and lifted it over his head, poised to slam it down.

The door started to open out, then paused. Through the low opening Hack saw one big black boot in the snow. Then a voice: "Who's in there?"

Hack relaxed. "A better question—who's out there?"

"Uncle Hack? Is that you?"

It was Little Gus.

18 *A House Is Not A Home*

A few moments later the two were relaxed in their wooden folding chairs, savoring the provisions Little Gus had carried in: small cheese-and-cracker packets, tortillas, dried fruit, beef jerky, protein bars, and two big delicious jars of peanut butter. "We'll save the instant potatoes and dry lentils and oatmeal for later," Gus said. "When we can heat them up."

"You travel well," Hack said. "Peanut butter on tortillas is a marriage made in heaven."

"Dad hides supplies all over. There's lots more. We'll never run out. He's like a squirrel, except he remembers every hole he hides his nuts."

"What are you doing in the woods and not at home?"

"You kidding? Dad told me what to do a long time ago. The instant I get the news he's arrested, I take off out of the house and into the woods. And maybe ten minutes later police and F.B.I. agents are swarming the place. I even see a helicopter." He grinned. "Of course, they never saw me."

"How'd you get the news?"

Little Gus shrugged. "Don't matter."

"Forget I asked. Sorry."

"No. It's okay. A friend sent a text. Like an alarm system Dad set up just in case."

"Just in case he got arrested?"

"Just in case just in case, I guess. You know my Dad."

"He's arrested, not you. Why are you hiding?"

"It's not just the cops. What about Family Services and the other busybodies? They'll take and stick me somewhere. I like it fine out here."

"What about school?"

"What about it?" Another teenage shrug.

Hack found himself shrugging back. What about school? "How

long are you planning to stay out here?"

"As long as it takes. I been keeping my eye on things. The cops have cleared out of our house. I'm going back to check it out tonight."

"They'll still be hunting for you. And every so often they'll drop back to the house just in case."

"Why, Uncle Hack. You know I'm always careful. And I had the best teacher."

This wasn't the right time to remind Little Gus his best teacher was locked up. "And you're sure the cops are gone from there for now?"

"Very sure. I'm heading back after dark. Want to come?"

"Why not?"

After dark the two booted their way to Gus's house. Hack wore his pack and carried his skis and poles on his shoulders.

No lights burned inside the white two-story frame house, but as the two approached, night time yard lights blazed from its front and back porches into the yard around.

"Motion triggered," said Little Gus. "See? We still got electricity."

"Won't someone see these lights?"

"They'll just think it's animals came near the house. Happens all the time."

They hiked up close. They ducked easily under the yellow crime scene tape circling the house and found the back door sealed:

"CRIME SCENE DO NOT ENTER"

Sealed by order of the Federal Bureau of Investigation.

Notice: breaking this seal without authorization is a crime under federal law.

YOU WILL BE PROSECUTED

"I know another way in," Little Gus said. "If we leave the tape intact and get in through a window, that's not a crime, is it?"

"I don't care."

"If you don't, I don't. And you're the grownup, right? Supposed to be leading me on the straight path?"

"If we're caught, I'll take the heat. They can tag an extra trespass sentence onto my murder sentences. And you can tell the judge it was just your dad's antisocial bad example. After all, you're a juvenile."

"That's always been my approach." Little Gus said, "And it's worked so far."

Hack followed Little Gus around the side of the house. Little Gus pointed out a low casement window. "Goes down into the basement," he said. "Never locked. Handy way in without drawing someone's attention."

"Someone like your dad?"

"Dad admires initiative. He tells me just don't get caught. If I get caught, then he punishes me. So I don't get caught."

Hack peered down at it. "Will I fit?"

"I always have."

"When was the last time?"

"Now that you mention, a couple years ago." Little Gus paused. "Or maybe longer."

"So you've put on what—maybe six inches and fifty pounds since then?"

"Maybe more. But it can't hurt to give it a shot." Little Gus bent down and pushed on the bottom of the window. It swung in on two small hinges at its top.

"Here we go," Little Gus said, and bent over. He gripped both sides of the wall around the window and sidled down feet first. Hack heard the thump of his feet on the concrete basement floor. A second later, Hack heard his voice. "Come on down. It still works for me. If I fit, you sure will."

Hack laid his skis and poles against the wall, took off his back pack and followed Little Gus's example. A moment later, he hit feet first on the concrete basement floor and rolled over, then popped to his feet.

"Pretty good," Little Gus said, and added, "For a geezer."

They both flicked on flashlights.

"Keep your fingers over the light to keep it dim," Little Gus said.

"Yeah," Hack said. "I've seen the same TV shows as you."

Little Gus led the way and Hack followed him up the basement stairs.

The house was a mess. Furniture was knocked on its side everywhere. Two plush chairs were actually broken apart, as if someone had bashed them against the walls. Dents and slash marks puckered the walls. Two coffee tables lay on their sides. Hack had drunk a lot of beers and watched a lot of games on the big living room sofa, but he would never get the chance again: the sofa was upside down, its stuffing torn out of it and spread over the floor.

Hack followed Little Gus into the kitchen, which suffered the same destruction.

"It's like Europe out of one of those World War Two documentaries," Little Gus said.

"I guess the police mean business," Hack said. "But do they have to tear things up like animals?"

"It's not the locals. We know most of them. Half of them have had a beer or two here as guests and friends. I bet it's the F.B.I. did this." Little Gus nodded. "They love to show off their power."

"I'm sorry they busted up your home, Little Gus. But it's cold in here and we've got the propane stove and a lot more safety back in the shack. Now that we've seen this, is there any point in our being here?"

"Might be." Little Gus led Hack down the corridor to his bedroom. The bed was tilted sideways as if a leg were missing. Somebody had cracked more holes in the walls and ripped out insulation and scattered the insulation all over.

Little Gus took a thin but bulky item out of his own pack. Hack recognized the salvaged laptop. "One thing we got here we don't have in the shack. Electricity." Little Gus plugged the laptop into an outlet. He sat on the floor and leaned back against the tilted bed and set the laptop on his thighs and turned it on.

Hack said, "I'd be surprised if they left your home network working."

Little Gus shook his head. "Seems you're behind the times again,

Uncle Hack."

"Would you please stop calling me Uncle?"

"Sure. As soon as you start calling me L.G. I'm bigger than Dad now anyway."

"I'll consider it."

Little Gus took a cartridge from his pocket and plugged it into he laptop. "We're just here for the electricity. Dad signed me up for a satellite network. Always available no matter where I go."

"That Gus."

"That Dad," Gus agreed.

"What are you after?" Hack asked.

"News, is all."

The only chair in the room was broken. There was nowhere to sit, so Hack found a relatively unscathed part of the wall and leaned back against it. "See anything?"

"The news hasn't changed. You're still a racist ogre and Dad's still locked up."

Hack said, "Maybe you can make something of this." He took the flash drive out of his pocked and handed it to Little Gus.

"What's that?"

"Read it and see."

Little Gus stuck the flash drive into a USB port on the side of the laptop. He clicked some keys and scanned the screen.

Hack watched the boy's face in the eerie light cast by the screen. Hack was standing in the father's old room with the son who was a clone of the Gus that Hack remembered hanging with in this very room years ago. But now the room was dark and cold and wrecked, and the boy's face illuminated only by the glow from an LCD screen.

"Say," Hack said. "You know Mattie pretty well, don't you?"

Little Gus glanced up. "Sure. Unusual lady. Dad calls her highly excitable. Sometimes he means it as a compliment, but I think she can scare even Dad once she gets wound up. But she's always been sweet to me. She used to come around a lot after my Mom took off. Little Gus considered a moment. "I haven't seen her much lately. Why?"

"Just asking. I ran into her the other day is all."

Little Gus continued looking up at him. In the dim light, Hack suspected a hint of speculation in the boy's expression.

Hack added, "And you know, she sings with my band."

"Right. Well, she did a lot for me back then. Really took care of me when my mom took off and I was small and I needed it a lot. Being older now and looking back, I guess maybe it was some kind of a connection she needed at the time too. You know."

"I know." Hack nodded. Then caught himself. "What do I know?"

"It was after her own girl died. You know. Her daughter. Teddi, I think."

"I didn't know Mattie has a daughter."

"Had. Drowned when she was two in some stupid accident at some lake. Tore Mattie up, Dad said."

"No, I didn't know any of that. This girl was Rennie's?"

"No. Before Rennie. I guess you weren't around at the time, so you don't know any of this, do you?"

"No, I don't. Although I suppose it would have been nice if someone had mentioned it sometime."

"I guess you got to ask someone sometime."

A fifteen-year-old was explaining basic human decency to him. Hack said, "I guess sometimes you do have to ask someone sometime."

Little Gus went back to his work at the laptop.

Hack said, "Hanging here with you reminds me of all the times I hung with your Dad when he was your age."

Little Gus stayed focused on the LCD screen. "That right?"

"Those were interesting times."

Little Gus keyed something, then read something more from the screen. "You don't say."

"I suppose your Dad never told you about some of the crazy stuff we did."

Still focused: "Umm."

"Old guy stuff might be pretty boring for you, I suppose."

"Might," Little Gus agreed. "But I suppose some of it could have happened." He finally looked at Hack. "That crazy stuff all must have been before you went away."

"Obviously."

"No, I mean before you went away and came back...you know."

Hack seemed to be piling one ignorance on top of another. "Now what don't I know?"

"You know." Little Gus shrugged his trademark teenage shrug as if reluctant to say it. Then he did anyway: "A dud."

"A dud."

"You know, like a wet firecracker. Or a round won't go off—no matter how hard the hammer or striker smacks it in the ass."

"I know what a dud is. Where'd you get that word?"

"Dad."

"Dad said 'dud'."

"Yep."

"My lifelong friend and companion called me a dud?"

"He told me I shouldn't ever repeat it to anyone, especially not you, but he couldn't totally blame Lily for dumping you. Then he used that word: 'dud'."

"Right around the time he told you not to repeat it?"

Little Gus nodded, now with a bright innocent smile. "Exactly that time."

"He doesn't blame Lily for dumping me?"

"Nah, You know, Uncle Hack, I'm not trying to be mean here. I'm kind of trying to do you a favor. You've been awful dull since you came back. Not like before. I remember you different. You were different. You were fun."

"Thanks a lot."

"You're welcome." With no apparent irony. "Word to the wise, you know. I mean, if you're interested in Mattie. Women like exciting guys."

"How do you know what women like?"

"I'm keeping an eye out. And maybe I don't and maybe I do. Anyway, we've definitely crossed into need-to-know territory here."

Little Gus went back to his clicking and reading while Hack stewed and pondered and wondered.

After about thirty interminable minutes, Little Gus leaned back against the bed. "I think I get the first part. It's history. Really ancient history. These Muslims dudes have got something against Jews. And the Muslims are all hot to conquer the world for Allah or something. Or so they say. 'Cause it seems like they do pretty damn well for themselves personally while they're fighting for their god, you know, grabbing the land and the women and the loot. But I'm not sure why you're showing me this."

"Someone murdered my friend Amir. I'm on the hook for it. They've locked up your dad. I'm trying to figure out what's going on. Maybe this Khaybar thing has something to do with it."

"Why would it?"

"I showed it to Amir right before he was murdered. He said he'd check it out."

"So?"

Hack told him about Amalki.

"Okay. And this Amalki's a Muslim too?"

"Seems likely. I never actually had the chance to ask. What about the second document? I can't make it out at all."

Little Gus leaned back and stretched his arms up and intertwined his hands behind his neck. "Oh, that's easy."

"Don't sit there looking smug. Tell me."

"It's like a game."

"How so?"

"Well, you know, in a game, sometimes they give you a list of things you have to acquire. Tools or jewels or a special sword or a magic phrase to figure out. Whatever. You need to gather those to overcome some obstacles and proceed to the next level in the game, whatever that level is."

"So this document is a list of things someone needs? What for?"

"Hard to say. Even after the translation from Arabic, it's still in some kind of code, I think. That's why it makes no sense."

"Can you crack it?"

"I'm just a kid, remember? You're the professional. Dad says you can do anything with computers. Isn't that why they call you Hack?"

"No. But I'm open to suggestions. And here's your chance to show up the decrepit geezer dud."

"I guess the fact it's coded in the first place tells us something. People don't code things for no reason, do they?"

"No. Any hints at all? Give me some help and you're 'LG' from now on."

"Fair enough. You see these words here?" Little Gus swiveled the laptop so that Hack could see its screen. "The words I highlighted?"

يـهـود

Hack leaned closer to see. "Okay."

"Well, we both think that's the Arabic word for Jews, right?"

"According to the translation websites."

Near that, I see this:

بـشفـة تـو

"Okay."

"And I see the same pair of words in Arabic over and over in this second document. Here, and here, and here. See?"

Hack leaned over again and confirmed. The same squiggles repeated over and over. "What does it mean in English?"

Little Gus swiveled the laptop back and clicked a few times and turned the screen back to show Hack:

Toe Lip

Hack said, "Toe lip."

Little Gus nodded. "Yep. Toe Lip." He nodded again, seeming satisfied with his discovery.

"So all I have to do is figure out what 'Toe Lip' means and I can solve Amir's murder and get myself off and get your Dad out of jail?"

"Could be. Maybe."

"What could go wrong? While I work that out, please copy everything on that drive into your lap top. Might be our only backup."

"Already did." LG pulled the flash drive out the lap top USB port and handed it back to Hack.

The two snuck out through the corridors, picking their way over and around debris to the basement stairs. In the basement they found an old dining room chair and propped it by the still open casement window. LG climbed onto the chair and grabbed the window frame and lifted himself up and through the window with an agility astonishing for someone his size. A moment later, Hack saw LG's big hands reaching down through the window. Hack stood on the chair and grabbed the hands. Hack and LG intertwined their hands and their arms wrist against wrist. "On three," said Little Gus, and they counted together. On three, Hack jumped and LG yanked. A moment later Hack bounced off LG and found himself sprawled on the cold ground.

LG lay back on the snow laughing. "Sweet." Then he scrabbled over and reached into the house to grab the window by the sides and pull it mostly shut. "That's as far as it'll go from the outside. Maybe no one will notice. And if they do? They'll think it was burglars or looters."

"I'm sorry about your house, LG. And the mess and your dad in jail. And everything else."

"Not your fault. It's the Feds. They hate Dad."

"Why?"

"Maybe because Dad hates them. Like Hatfields and McCoys."

The two stood and brushed the snow off each other. Hack put on his back pack and hoisted his skis and pole. They hiked back towards the woods. As they passed the shed, Hack had an inspiration. "One more thing."

LG stopped. "Yeah?"

"Let's see if the feds left the Fox behind."

The two entered the shed through the side door and clicked on their flashlights and played their beams over the little red Audi Fox, which sat facing the front door cold, forlorn and dead in the otherwise dark shed.

"They sailed right past it," Hack said.

"It's just a wreck."

"So they thought."

"What'd my Dad say was wrong?"

"Cracked distributor cap."

"That's all?"

"Sure."

"That reminds me." LG played his beam around the shed, went over to shelf and pulled something down. He held it up for Hack to see: a package. "He had a new cap overnighted. Twenty bucks from Bosch Auto Parts. You can pay us later. He hadn't got around to installing it before they grabbed him."

"Can you install it?"

"Sure."

"You've done it?"

"No, but I've helped Dad. At least a dozen times. Happens all the time with these local beaters."

"It's not a beater."

"Of course not. Or a clunker."

"Nope."

"Or a junker."

"I think a Junker is some kind of Kraut."

"As in food?"

"Never mind."

LG asked, "Was that a joke?"

"What if it was?"

"That's the first real joke I've heard out of you since you came back. Before you left you were always fun and I was really an excited kid every time you were going to come over and hang out. You know, joking around and playing games and everything. You were like another kid yourself."

"Before I got to be such a dud?"

"Right. Now that I think about it, this whole time tonight you're my old Uncle Hack again. Sneaking in your snarky wise cracks. Like we're Butch and Sundance in that old movie."

"So?"

"So I guess the life of a hunted fugitive suits you."

"Lucky for me," Hack said. "How long to fix the Fox?"

"Maybe an hour to do the job right. Ninety minutes tops. Get in, pop the hood and then get out and hold the light for me. And we'll take out the battery and charge it while I make the switch."

"I'll need gas."

"We've got gas, naturally."

"Naturally."

Ninety minutes later, Hack drove the fully fueled Fox out of the shed and stopped to wait while LG closed the shed doors behind him. The Fox idled smooth and perfect. Like new. Maybe better than new.

LG walked over and stood beside the driver side window. "You know where you're going?"

"Yes. But it's better you don't."

"Makes sense. Don't forget about getting Dad out."

"Of course I won't. He's your dad, but he's also my friend. The best friend this geezer dud ever had." Hack stuck his left arm out through the window. LG clasped Hack's hand in his own left. Then he bumped the top of their joined left hands with the bottom of his right fist.

"Is that one of those new handshakes?"

"Sometimes I make up my own." LG let go. "Here's something that may help." He handed Hack a package wrapped in brown paper and backed away two steps.

Hack tore open the wrapping. A sheathe. He pulled the clean steel out of the sheathe. "Gus's Kabar."

"I think Dad would want to lend it to you while he's locked up. I heard they took yours."

"Many thanks."

"Something you can use when you get to the next level."

Hack said, "If I get to the next level."

"You will."

As Hack pulled up the gravel drive and away from the white old house, he checked his rear-view mirror and saw LG watching him for a moment. Then LG waved and turned his back and began his trek into the woods and its deeper and safer darkness.

19 Computer Science

Hack headed for the Ojibwa College campus. That's where the Khaybar computer had come from. A college campus was a big place to search for whoever wrote the Khaybar letter, but he could think of no alternative.

Since it was still winter break, it might be reasonably safe. Likely there wouldn't be too many people on campus, especially now in the late night hours. He checked the clock on the dashboard. Three A.M.. Plenty of time before morning, although he didn't yet have any specific idea how to use that time.

But for the first time since the Friday morning divorce papers, Hack felt some smidgen of control over his life. It was a small but genuine comfort to drive his own car down a familiar road he had driven a thousand times towards the town he'd grown up in. In that tiny town he knew every street and every house and most of the people who lived in those houses. Of course, with the passage of time some had died and some had moved and otherwise been replaced by new people. But he nursed a reasonable hope they were the same kind of people, the kind who would snub the F.B.I. as long as they presumed Hack innocent. People like Mattie and LG and all the others at Berringer's.

And like Amir too. Hack felt a new stab of sorrow and regret at the loss of Amir. In the same circumstances Amir would have been just as close-mouthed as his other neighbors. Maybe more, given their friendship and Amir's natural reticence—as well as his upbringing under Saddam Hussein's vicious dictatorship.

Whatever was going on wasn't just about Hack. Other people were suffering. Better people. Gus was locked up, LG was wandering fatherless in the winter woods, Amir had been butchered, and Mattie--

Mattie? What about Mattie? He'd had eight months to pay her some decent attention before he hid out in her home and scarfed her food and hopped into her bed. In those eight months he might have troubled to discover the trivial item that she'd had a baby who drowned.

No doubt—he was a self-centered jerk. In a spasm of frustration he pounded a fist on the steering wheel. The Fox went into a brief skid and he had to struggle to steer it to stay on the road—barely.

Not only self-centered, but a klutz.

He cruised down the nearly empty County 15 and then down the empty side streets and found a parking spot on a plowed side street half a block from the campus. In case he had to leave in a hurry, he parked facing away from the campus and towards County 15. He left his back pack in the trunk and grabbed a few portable items he guessed might come in handy. Then he walked through the darkness onto the campus.

He wandered among the dark buildings, not sure what he was looking for. It was easy going. The campus sidewalks and paths were plowed. The temperature was about 20 degrees Fahrenheit, a decent warm spell by Minnesota January standards. He was dressed for the cold anyway, so he felt no discomfort.

In fact, he might have been overdressed. Having his ski mask down over his face might have drawn unwelcome attention from locals, who regarded weather like this as positively balmy. Nevertheless, in case he ran into someone, he kept the face mask down as he prowled among the silent and dark campus buildings. But he saw nobody anyway.

One or two signs identified each building. Some hung on the buildings and some were posted in front. Ojibwa College seemed to teach a lot of "Studies": "Peace Studies," "Intercultural Studies"; "Renewable and Sustainable Studies"; and "Feminist Studies".

Just past the "Feminist Studies" building, there was another building labeled "Advanced Feminist Studies."

He wondered whether students of mere "Feminist Studies" felt they were being short changed.

"Musical Studies." What was that? the musician in Hack wondered. All music is studying. In fact, music had been the only thing he ever studied in his own college career, even obsessively—to the point where his over-practicing led to repetitive stress syndrome and agony in his right wrist.

Since then he'd dropped his obsession with music. Why? Was it the peanuts they paid him to play? Something to do with his marriage to Lily and the arrival of Sarai?

Maybe it was around that same time he turned into a dud.

One sign stopped him short in momentary wonder: "Chemistry, Physics, Geology and Other Physical Sciences."

They still teach those? Well that's something. But they cram it all into a little brick one-story building.

"Computer Science." In college, Hack had not even so much as audited a single computer science class, but afterwards he had managed to pry a good living out of computers—for a while.

He pondered the building's possibility. Maybe get access to better hardware and software? The building was sure to provide more powerful tools for correlating search results.

He saw a glass door by the side of the building. He approached it and gave the handle a gentle pull. Locked, naturally.

If Gus were here, he could pick that lock in twenty seconds. But he wasn't. Just in case, Hack had brought the burglar tools out of the Gus Go Bag. Should he give it a try? Did he have any better ideas?

He pulled up his ski mask and pressed his face close to the glass and peered in. Beyond the glass door there was an alcove and on the other side of the alcove stood another door. It was too dark inside to make out much. Some kind of big man-sized bundle lay on the floor by the inside door. An oversized mail bag? No, too big. And blankets covered it.

Hack tugged on the outside door again. This time it rattled. The big bundle stirred. The round figure of a man sat up. He must have heard Hack. He stared at the door. The man got to his feet and stepped up to the door and pressed a bearded face against it. The man's face flattened and distorted against the glass.

Hack back pedaled like a defensive back and turned to sprint away. The door flung open. "Mr. Hack?"

It was Homeless Hal.

"Come on in, Mr. Hack."

"You sure?"

"Sure. I'm the only one around."

"Well, okay."

Hal held the door open and Hack stepped in. As he passed Hal, Hack caught Hal's distinct powerful musky aroma. It was Hal, all right.

Once Hack was through the outer door, Hal scrambled past him and grabbed his blankets up from the floor and then opened the inner door, which was unlocked. Hack followed Hal into the building.

Hal said, "There's machines."

"What?

"Machines. You know."

"No, sorry. I don't."

"Machines. You know. With chips."

Hack looked at Hal. "Chips? This is the Computer Science Building, right?"

As if addressing a two-year-old, Hal now enunciated with great care, "Are you hungry, Mr. Hack? You look hungry."

"Actually, yes." Hack had gone long hours since sharing LG's wonderful provisions in the shack.

"Machines. Come on. I'll show you." Hal led Hack down dark corridors with the sure confidence of a scout who knew his territory. Hack followed Hal into a big open room with dozens of tables and chairs—obviously a cafeteria. Vending machines lined the walls like silent robot sentinels in the darkness on the right.

"Machines," Hal said. "Chips. Potato. Corn. Original, too, not those weird spicy flavors like they got now. Also candy bars. Soup to heat up. Food." Then, abruptly: "You got money?"

"Yeah." But Hack remembered he had left the Gus Go Bag cash along with most of his other supplies in the trunk of the Fox.

"Or maybe." Hack fumbled in his pocket.

Hal waited with serene patience.

Hack found his wallet and pulled it out and took out some bills. He held them up for Hal's inspection.

"Excellent," Hal said.

The two headed for the machines. A few minutes later, Hack was admitting to himself that under the right circumstances corn chips and chemically softened cookies and a Milky Way could make a tasty meal, even if he downed them with bitter black vending machine coffee.

Hack did pause a moment to inspect and sniff the coffee after the machine poured it into a paper cup.

Three weeks into the winter break. It might have been every one of those three weeks since they refilled this machine with new makings.

Then he decided to take the chance. Couldn't be worse than Starbuck's.

He was right. Even a bit better. And one buck instead of five.

After their meal, Hal leaned back in his cafeteria chair and folded his hands over his considerable paunch. He belched, then giggled like a little girl caught doing something naughty. He smiled at Hack as he picked his teeth with a tooth pick he pulled from his pocket.

Hack asked, "Hal, it's none of my business, but what are you doing here?"

"What I do everywhere."

"But why do that here?"

"Got to do somewhere." The Zen Master.

"Why on the campus in particular?"

"People take special care of me here. Mrs. Malkin's really nice and a few of the other ladies are too, but I like to spread myself around." Then, with a roguish air, "Don't want to limit myself to just one lady. Or impose too long."

"What about imposing on the college?"

Hal shook his head. "They're not my friends. Not like you. It makes them feel good to give me stuff. So let them."

Hal's tiny blue eyes glinted over his red bearded cheeks. He tilted his head forward and leaned towards Hack. "You hiding out?"

"What?"

"How come I got to say everything twice to you, Mr. Hack? You used to get things the first time. You hiding out?"

"Everybody seems to know my business."

"What everybody knows, I know," Hal said. "If you're hiding out, I'm good at hiding. I got skills. I can teach you. You done eating?"

Hack nodded.

Hal said, "Come on." He stood and waved his thick arm to follow. He led Hack down a hall to a stairway. Hack got around to asking the obvious question. "This building's locked, Hal. How did you get in?"

"I get into a lot of buildings on campus."

"A lot?"

"Most."

They took the stairs leading down. Hack followed Hal into a locker room. "A change of clothes," Hal said. "You maybe could use one."

Hal yanked open an unlocked door of one of the lockers. "Dress like me," he said. "You can go anywhere. No one will see you. No one sees me."

Hack took a sniff at the clothing in the locker, then a second deeper one. "I don't know."

"You're on the run, right?"

"Right."

"So be homeless. You can go anywhere, at least outdoors. Everyone looks away. They stare at the ground or up in the sky. No eye contact. They're afraid you're going to talk to them or drool on them or do the scariest thing of all and ask for money."

"Makes sense."

Hal continued his tutorial. "Looks like you've stopped trimming your beard—good start there. If you mumble to yourself nonstop or carry on both sides of a conversation real loud, works even better."

"Those are good tips."

Hal nodded in self-satisfaction. "You bet. Very good tips. A man hiding out can learn a lot from me. Now take the clothes and put them on."

Hack started to take off his clothes. "What about mine? Shouldn't we figure out a way to get rid of them? Burn them or something?"

Hal said, "No problem. Once I've worn them, no one'll want them."

Hack took off everything but his underwear and dropped it all on the floor. Outer garment by outer garment, he put on what Hal handed him out of the locker. As Hack did so, he transferred contents from the pockets of his old clothes to his new.

Hal removed his own clothes and stuffed them in the locker. Then he put on Hack's.

"Tight around the waist," Hal said. "And the sleeves are too short. But that just adds to the look."

Hack examined Hal. They were almost identical in height, but Hal was bigger round--a rotund ginger scarecrow. Hack asked, "You think I look homeless?"

As soon as Hack asked the question, the hard truth hit home. He was homeless. For real. More homeless even than Hal.

Hal gave a big grin and shot him a thumbs up. "And you smell homeless, too."

Hack made a mental note: shower before the next time he saw Mattie. If there was a next time. That thought brought with it another stab of misery.

Hack shoved the misery aside and tried to focus. Hal's brag suggested another idea: "You said you could get into almost any building?"

"Sure."

"How?"

"Depends on the building."

"Okay," Hack said. "Somewhere on this campus they bought some new computers and threw out the old ones. Did you see anything like that? Do you have any idea what building that was?"

"No, sorry. I'm only here part time, you know. I got rounds to make."

"Understood. But the people who threw out those computers

might have taught courses in history or religion or history of religion or something like that. Does that help?"

"What religion?"

"Well, it could have been any. The Jewish religion. Or Islam. Or even Christianity. Or all of them together somehow."

"All those religions and histories together."

"Yes. Like that."

Hal gave a slow nod. "In one place?"

"Yes, all in one place. Maybe."

Hal's tiny bright blue eyes glowed from his round cheeks. "I think I know that place. Come on."

Hal led Hack out through the same door he had used to let Hack in. They walked in the darkness about fifty yards down a path to another building. An illuminated sign hung over the front door:

Department of Mideast Studies

Hal said, "Down here." He passed the front door and led Hack to a side entrance set lower in the side of the building and down a wheelchair ramp. "Usually locked, but not too well." He banged one giant mittened fist against a spot on the metal framing of the button. Nothing. He banged it twice more. Then he pressed the button. The door swung out open. "See?"

"I do see. Very good."

Hal asked, "What time is it?"

"I haven't got a watch or a phone that's on, but I guess about six A.M.."

"Sounds about right. Far as I go. It'll be sunrise soon. I'll head back to Mrs. Malkin's. Like to get there safe in the dark before it turns light. Fewer hassles."

"I can give you a ride, if you need one."

"It's three blocks."

"Okay." Then as Hal started to turn away, another rush of emotion gripped Hack. "So long, Hal," he said. He grabbed Hal and hugged him. It was like hugging a padded beer barrel. Hack's hands did not meet on Hal's other side. "You really are a friend."

"Mr. Hack, you never showed this much emotion before. In fact, I never seen you show any emotion at all."

"You're a good man, Hal."

"That's fine now, Mr. Hack." Hal patted Hack's arm and disentangled himself and gave Hack a gentle shove away. "Time I go my way. And you go yours."

"You're right."

Hal walked back up the ramp and turned left and disappeared.

Hack walked through the door Hal had sprung open. The door closed behind him.

20 MidEast Studies

Hack stood at the end of a long corridor. Pointed where? It was now Wednesday morning, and for the first time since Saturday night and Amir's murder Hack felt stirrings of hope. This very instant he might be standing only a few yards from the place the discarded computer and its Khaybar document came from. And maybe these connected somehow to Amir's murder and the mess Hack was in.

And maybe not. It was a thin chain of inference.

Visibility was poor. There were low night lights every few yards. They illuminated the tiled floor and the lower portions of the walls and nothing much above. He took a small flashlight out of his coat pocket and flicked it on and moved into the darkness. The memory of LG's advice to keep his fingers over the light brought a smile to his face. He followed the advice anyway.

Waste no time. If it really were six in the morning, people might start arriving soon, even during the winter break.

He passed a bulletin board. Stapled to it were some small notices about upcoming presentations, including one entitled "Exposing Bias: Islamophobia and the Media."

Next to the notice he saw a twelve-inch-by-twelve-inch map labeled in big blue and white letters: "The Future of Zionism." The map was missing the small Mideast countries Hack normally saw. The map replaced them with a giant blue and white Israel that occupied Egypt, Iran, Turkey and the entire Arabian Peninsula. Hack got the message: the Jews wanted the whole middle east.

To the right of the map right Hack saw a poster about twelve inches by twenty, with big black letters on a yellow background:

**Support the International Call
for Boycott, Divestments and Sanctions**
ON ISRAEL

Next to the poster someone had pinned a small color photo. A crew of about a dozen proud grinning demonstrators held a giant yellow banner that sported black letters in the same font as the poster's: "BOYCOTT APARTHEID ISRAEL."

Hack played his flashlight beam on the small photo and peered up close. One of the faces might have been Amalki's. Another might have been Daghestani.

Hack resumed his walk down the corridor. He read the name plate on each door he passed: "Sonia Salito, Tayeb Chahuan, Mohammed Mokdis, Stu Isaacson, Jabbar Domki…" So far he saw no name he recognized.

Some doors had small posters or notes. One cartoon caught his eye. A disappointed Uncle Sam pointed to a clunker of an auto labelled "Iraq War" steaming in ruin behind him. A used car salesman in a loud checker coat bearing the insignia "Zionist Lobby" was pointing proudly behind himself to a shiny new vehicle labelled "Iran War." The Zionist salesman explained to Uncle Sam, "Forget about that clunker I sold you yesterday. I got something much sweeter for you today."

On another door was taped a small clipping from a magazine:

ISIS=CIA=MOSSAD

More Proof That ISIS is a creation of Zionism

One door on the right after that, Hack finally recognized a name. Hack read: "Tariq Daghestani." Below that, it said "Adjunct Scholar."

Hack had no idea what an "Adjunct Scholar" was. But this was Lily's new client and a spokesman for the upcoming "Rock The Unity." A once-over of his office seemed a good idea. It was the only idea he had anyway.

Hack tried the door—locked. No Hal this time. But thanks to Gus, Hack had an alternative. He pulled the small packet of burglar tools from the Gus Go Bag out of his pocket.

It had been years since Hack used them. As twelve-year-olds, he and Gus had invented what they considered history's most original prank. One midnight Hack snuck out of his house and met Gus in the alley behind Meriwether Hardware. Gus taught Hack how to use burglar tools to pick the back-door lock. Where Gus acquired his skill went unexplained.

The two boys snuck inside the store. The store's paint and plumbing aisles were exactly the same length and height. They spent three hours exchanging every item on the paint aisle with every item on the adjoining plumbing aisle and vice versa. To assure perfection, the boys took "before" Polaroid snapshots of each aisle. Applying more painstaking care than either ever gave his school homework, they made sure each item's new location precisely matched its old one. Afterwards they took souvenir photos and retreated to Hack's basement to admire them.

Eight forty-five A.M. sharp the next morning, Hack and Gus were first in line in front of the store, two junior scientists keen to observe the results of their experiment. When Mr. Meriwether opened at nine, they were the first through the door. They nudged and giggled their way over to their trick aisles. They were eager to savor the inevitable delicious adult over-reaction.

Which never came. Mr. Meriwether never twitched an eyebrow. The boys tried dropping a few hints, like "Say, Mr. Meriwether, where's the latex?" or "Does this plunger seem different somehow?"

He just repeated, "How can I help you boys?" his fixed storekeeper smile painted on.

Finally, the boys pooled two dollars and bought a small jar of brown paint and trudged away in sullen disappointment.

It took a few weeks for Hack to think back and identify the winning prankster.

The prank had flopped but Hack hoped the skills stayed with him. The tool set included several picks, each with a long handle and a short narrow blade with a hooked end. He inserted one into the keyhole, then wiggled it. When that failed, he tried another. In a few minutes he found the right pick and the door's cheap lock gave in. Hack opened the door and went inside and then shut the door behind him as quietly as he could.

Hack shone the flashlight beam around the small office. A swivel chair sat in front of a gray metal desk. A keyboard lay on the desk in front of a dark computer screen. Hack checked it out—the latest high-powered model—a likely replacement for a discarded desk top.

Book shelves lined the walls. The shelves were mostly empty, which surprised Hack, but maybe Daghestani came here only part time. All the books were in English. The books included "The Language of Baklava," which seemed to be about food, and "Lipstick Jihad," which seemed to be about women, and "I Shall Not Hate" about a Gazan doctor.

A small clock on a shelf read 6:20 A.M..

Hack spotted another other book on the desk next to the keyboard. Hack picked it up. It was in Arabic—the only book in Arabic. But the hand-written note taped to it was in English. The note was in green ink on lavender stationery with the printed heading "Department of Advanced Intersectionalist Studies":

> "Tariq—
> "Thanks so much for the chance to read this. It justifies all the many long hours I spent in Qatar improving my Arabic. More importantly, it has given me a different perspective well worth exploring, even if I cannot find myself in total consonance with all I read there. I am continually working on myself. Thanks to your kind and conscientious tutelage, I am now better able to grapple with the Orientalist mindset I absorbed in my upbringing. I recognize that not every value, belief and perspective I was taught to hold precious can control across every continent, era and culture. I must try to learn from you—"
> With respect and friendship (I hope),
> Sonia"

Must be quite a book. Hack sat down in the desk chair and powered up the desk top. Happily, he needed no password to get into the system. Unhappily, this meant the computer likely held no secrets. Hack quickly navigated to the Arabic translation website he knew from before.

He had nothing to copy and paste—so he had to type in the words. But how type in Arabic? The desk top keyboard was in English. By playing with the site, he found he could make the site display a small picture of an Arabic keyboard. By maneuvering the mouse arrow Arabic lettered keys and pressing "Enter" he entered Arabic letters into the site.

He entered what he thought was the first letter of the book's title, then the second one. More frustration: Arabic went right to left instead of left to right like English.

In his left hand he held the book up next to the screen and with his right hand started keying in the letters as best he could from the book cover. The process was painful. He couldn't distinguish one letter from another. Often his first try was wrong. Repeatedly he had to erase a letter he'd misread. More frustration—he discovered the delete arrow quite logically followed the Arabic language and moved opposite to the direction he was used to: left to right instead of right to left. By habit, he kept deleting in the wrong direction.

The laborious process of entering three words in Arabic cost Hack a precious twenty-five minutes, but finally he could compare the book with the screen and think he had transcribed all three words correctly into the site's box for Arabic:

كفــا حي

هتـلـر أد ولـف

Hack pressed the enter key and saw the translation:

Mein Kampf
Adolf Hitler

Hack had not thought his opinion of college professors could sink. Now it plummeted. "A different perspective well worth exploring"?

Hack thought, not fair. This Sonia is probably not representative. Is she? Of course not. But that depends on the department and the school, doesn't it?

Or maybe she meant something other than the obvious. Something very sophisticated and appropriate to high level intersectionalist discourse.

Of course, if Daghestani had lent her this book for her edification, that said something bad about him. No way around that.

Hack turned off the monitor and computer and got up from the desk. He laid the book exactly as he remembered having found it, the thank-you note facing up.

He turned off the flashlight and opened the door and looked both ways down the hall. No one coming from either direction.

He headed back down the corridor towards the door through which he'd entered. Then he heard a noise. From the same door. Two men talking.

A short half-flight of steps led up a stairwell to a dark landing where there was a double door. He scooted up into the inky darkness and turned and squatted down in his baseball catcher's position. Behind him was a door to the outside. The door had a bar across it, the kind that was hinged to the door. He'd only have to push the bar.

The voices grew louder.

The men stopped in the corridor somewhere near his hiding place but still out of sight. They seemed to be arguing in a foreign language he didn't recognize. One of them asked a brief question. The other replied with a short bark that had the ring of a negative.

They came closer and repeated what might have been the identical exchange.

Then one of them spoke in English. "Do we have to speak Arabic? Your Arabic offends my ears. For one thing, your accent."

Hack thought he recognized the voice.

The other said, "As does yours offend mine, with its wretched grammar and crude street expressions. Surely, the Prophet never intended his tongue to be distorted into such noise."

The other laughed. "We agree, then." His buddy laughed back. Friendly joshing.

The two men moved again, then stopped almost directly down the half-flight of stairs from Hack. The dim light coming up from the corridor night lights gave a weird cast to their faces. But Hack recognized Amalki for sure. Amalki was facing his partner, who faced towards him and away from Hack.

This other man was shorter and his back was wide and muscular. Hack had seen and heard Daghestani only once and that had been only on television. He could be Daghestani.

Amalki gave a loud sniff. He said, "I'm sure I smell something."

"Maybe one of the Mujahid's Khaffir colleagues left some barbecued pork and it rotted. It's been three weeks since any of them dropped by to pretend to work." The man seemed amused.

Hack was not amused. He was wearing Hal's clothes—riper than any three-week old barbecue.

"No," Amalki said. "It's not food. It's much worse. Like the worst beggar on the foulest streets of al-Quds."

"A place you have never been."

"But I will be. Soon." Amalki said. "And as the Khaffir spread their misery everywhere in our world they make beggars of our people everywhere they go."

Amalki sniffed again, then swiveled with the athletic ease Hack recognized from the night at the Madhouse. "It seems strongest coming from up there." He glanced up into the stairwell at the spot directly over where Hack crouched. But the man gave no sign he saw Hack.

Hack froze and held his breath and hoped the darkness would protect him. His cramped legs began to ache—a long time since high school baseball.

Had he really taken practical advice from Hal? Some disguise.

The other grunted. "You want to snoop through all the offices for beggars or spoiled haram? Be my guest." His glance followed Amalki's up into the stairwell as well. Hack saw his face. The man was not Daghestani.

For an infinity all three men remained motionless. Then Amalki's gaze passed on. He turned and walked back in the direction from which he had come. Hack heard his footsteps move away, then become louder again as he returned to his friend.

"The smell's weaker back there," Amalki said.

"We really don't have time for this," the other said. "Let's finish our tee-bee-ess business with him and get on the move before people show up."

"'TBS'—that's the name you came up with?"

"I choose not to pronounce their language, although I was forced to learn words and phrases growing up. It is a jargon fit only for apes and pigs. What about you?"

"I cannot," Amalki said. "And I have no intention to learn. When they resume their natural Dhimmi status—the few of them who survive—they will learn to mangle ours again as best they can."

The two men resumed their way down the corridor in their original direction. The sound of their footsteps receded.

Hack exhaled and inhaled and started to straighten up. As he did, his cramped legs locked on him. His balance failed. He felt the door's metal bar behind him punch his lower back. The door gave and sprang open. The metal door hit the outside brick wall of the building with a clang. Hack fell backwards out into the chill air and staggered several steps before righting himself.

Hack knew in an instant he was in trouble. He took off down the first path he saw. He ran as if his life depended on it. Judging by the angry shouts behind him, it did.

21 Now What?

Hack's first thought was to run for the Fox, but he was cut off. He'd parked it on the other side of the campus. And every stride took him farther away.

He turned left down a sidewalk and glanced back and saw Amalki. Amalki ran with a cell phone in his hand—must be coordinating with his partner.

Amalki ran easy, like it was nothing to him. Hack was in shape, but he knew that in a foot race running fitness beats skiing fitness every time.

Hack saw an alley and turned into it. Black leafless branches stirred in the dim light of back yards on both sides. Hack heard Amalki shout something from behind. Hack's thighs began to stiffen. He slowed to a jog and hunted for a place to hide. There were garages by the alley, but all their doors seemed closed. Anyway, he'd be trapped in one of those.

He passed the Malkin house and through the glass back porch window caught a glimpse of a wide moving shadow.

Hack jogged another few dozen yards. He saw Amalki's partner at the other end of the alley. The man was peering into the open door of a garage and didn't seem to notice Hack. Hack glanced behind and saw Amalki striding from the other end of the alley. Amalki spoke into his phone. Ahead of Hack, Amalki's partner lifted his own phone and replied into it.

Hack ducked into a yard, desperate for friendly deeper darkness. He headed into the black space separating two houses. He crouched down and turned back to look towards the alley and saw his two pursuers converge there.

Amalki shouted, "Khaled! This way." He made a sweeping gesture with his right arm.

"I thought I saw him go into this yard."

"No. I know where he's hiding. He took shelter on a back porch.

Come." Amalki returned down the alley. Khaled followed.

What was that about? But a lucky break.

Hack hunkered down in his dark space between the houses, breathing deep and fast. Should he grab his chance and take off?

Then it hit him. He straightened up and raced back towards the Malkin house. He didn't bother with the alley, but crossed one back yard after another. He crashed through a low hedge and fell face first into a pile of snow and clambered upright and resumed his dash.

Through a window he saw the struggle on the Malkin back porch: three dark figures in a terrible dance. Hack recognized Amalki's quick serpentine movements. The squat broad figure was Khaled. So the wide one with his arms upraised in futile defense must be Hal.

As Hal fell, his scream echoed through the night.

Hack ran forward. Just before he arrived Amalki and Khaled fled like ghosts through the back door of the porch into the yard and then on towards the campus.

Hack heard one of them laugh. Khaled shouted, "Finally! The Khaffir Wilder down."

Amalki waved a black stick a few inches long. "I grabbed this from his pocket!"

The two disappeared down the alley into the early morning light.

Chasing the two of them was futile and likely fatal—Hack had no weapon. He stopped and bent over and put his hands on his hips and wheezed and gasped for oxygen.

He felt in his right front pants pocket. Nothing there. Where was the flash drive? He must have left it in his pocket when he and Hal exchanged clothes. Now Amalki had it.

One more screw-up.

Hack dreaded to look but he had to see. He straightened himself and limped up the steps to the porch, dragging one heavy leg after the other.

Hal lay on his back, his big coat rent open to reveal the red blood smearing his orange sweatshirt. He didn't move. The whiskers of his ginger beard curled dull and stiff and lifeless against his nearly white face. His wide open pale blue eyes stared upwards.

From within the house came the sound of a door opening. A light came on.

Hack stumbled out through the outside porch door and down the steps into the back yard. He started off on a roundabout way back to the Fox.

He heard Mrs. Malkin scream behind him.

Hack shuffled down the sunny morning sidewalk.

It was time he recognized the terrible truth about himself. He was incompetent—as useless as Mattie had said.

He should turn himself in. He'd get Sam for his lawyer. Sam was the smartest guy he'd ever met. Maybe Sam was smart enough to figure out what was going on. And smart enough to keep any more decent people from being killed.

He thought, I'm a carrier. Like Typhoid Mary. I hurt everyone I come near. Everyone. Amir, Gus, Little Gus, and now Hal. They should hang a bell around my neck to warn people away.

Even hapless Sven, a man Hack had never even heard of. Sven's mistake was generosity—providing the neighborhood a free open wireless network so Hack could blunder along and bring the cops down on him and wreck his business.

Hack should turn himself in and end all the misery he was carrying.

And what about Mattie?

Mattie.

The sun was up and people were already out and about. Soon more people would be moving around. Hack upped his tempo to a walking speed as brisk as he thought he could get away with and turned down the sidewalk which would take him to Mattie's.

He passed a lady walking her slightly obese schnauzer. The woman waited with a clear plastic bag over her right glove while her short stout companion snuffled around some bushes by the sidewalk. The Schnauzer sported doggy boots over its paws and a knitted blue sweater over its gray and white fur. It seemed a happy little mutt, absorbed in critical canine business, oblivious to all the irrelevant human distress in its vicinity.

The dog's lady nodded and said, "Good morning," but Hack just gave a nod and moved on.

Twenty minutes later he stood about a hundred yards from Mattie's on the opposite side of the street. On the outside everything seemed normal. Hack saw no police cars in the vicinity, but he wasn't sure the authorities needed a physical presence for surveillance.

He circled her block twice. No sign of anything out of the ordinary. A few trucks and cars were parked on the street. Lights were on in most of the houses. A middle-aged man with gray hair and a mustache came out of a house and walked to a rusted red pickup parked on the street. He got in and started up his pickup and drove away.

Hack passed Sven's Coffee House again. Closed. Yellow police tape still marked it off. Poor bastard.

Hack crossed the street and ducked under the tape and moved behind Sven's. He crouched on the cold courtyard bricks in the shadows under the canopy near the back wall. He removed his mittens and took a virgin cell phone out of his coat pocket and turned it on and waited for service. When the bars appeared, he dialed Mattie's number. No answer. He tried again. Still no answer.

So what now?

He turned off the phone and walked over to a trash bin intending to toss the phone, then rethought. He found a loose brick in the courtyard paving. He removed his mittens and pried the brick up with ease. He set the phone in the vacated spot and smashed the brick down on it time after time until the phone was debris. He lay the brick down on top of the debris and tried to adjust the brick to fit just as it had fit before. That might or might not slow them down.

Hack moved across the street towards Mattie's house. The chill air he breathed through his ski mask told him the temperature was plummeting towards zero again.

It was one of those deceptively sunny Minnesota January mornings. Someone gazing through her window could imagine she was looking at a lovely summer day—except for the snow piled everywhere and the knowledge won from hard experience that the frigid air could freeze your fingers and ears solid in a few careless minutes.

At least Hack could keep his ski mask down over his face and no one would think it odd.

He marched through Mattie's back yard up to the back door like he owned the place.

Time for a new mindset.

Running didn't work. Hiding didn't work. He needed a different approach. Charge ahead and charge right in.

Call it logic or call it rage, he now knew he wasn't going to turn himself in. He was going to drive forward and take his chances. What worse thing could happen?

He tried the back door. It opened. He went in.

A replay of Gus Dropo's house. The first furniture Hack saw was the kitchen table, broken as if a big weight had fallen on it. Someone had knocked over the chair where Hack had sat down to breakfast on Mattie's frozen pizza—how long?—just forty-eight hours ago.

Hack opened a kitchen drawer and grabbed a big chopping knife and held it blade upwards close to his side. He made a silent quick tour among the debris scattered through the house, careful with his boots not to step on or even nudge anything. He checked room by room, walking as slow and quiet as he could. No one there. The computer he'd given Mattie was gone.

But Hack saw a red smear about six inches by two on the door sill to Mattie's room. Someone had sprayed or spilled blood about shoulder high. It was only a single stain, but blood for sure. A quick touch with his bare finger told Hack it was dry. He knew he'd seen no blood on that wall two mornings ago.

He slipped back to the kitchen and wiped off the knife with a paper towel and stuffed the towel in his pocket. He replaced the knife in its drawer and glided out the back door to the sidewalk.

He took a roundabout route and ambled towards the Fox as if on a morning constitutional. He maintained a steady mechanical pace. He couldn't imagine anything or anyone that could stop him from getting where he was going.

It was Wednesday morning. Tonight was "Rock The Unity." So Hack knew where Adjunct Scholar and community activist "Mein Kampf" Daghestani was going to be. It wasn't hard to figure Daghestani knew something about the murders of Ahmed Abadi and Amir. And it would be history's smallest coincidence if Amalki and Khaled popped up in Daghestani's vicinity.

MinneCentre would be the ideal place to hunt them all up. Or down.

Hack had ditched that kitchen knife from Mattie's kitchen drawer because he didn't need it. He had a much bigger and better and more lethal knife in his pack in the trunk of his Fox.

The Kabar.

22 *The Big Town*

Early that afternoon, Hack parked near the Mississippi River on a side street about a mile from the MinneCentre. He strolled along the river towards the complex, in no particular hurry to get there. The concert was hours away. He needed time to come up with a plan anyway. And he was hungry.

Which seemed strange. For months he'd never felt any hunger. Now he couldn't stop eating. Did fear and confusion and rage make you hungry? Or did some unconscious part of him crave fuel for the big job ahead?

Sleep when you can and eat when you can, his father said.

When he lived in St. Paul he had often driven by a shelter near the Centre. There were always clusters of indigent men and women standing around in front, chatting and smoking. He had never gone inside, but he assumed the destitute gathered there for meals.

He walked left on Eagle Parkway northward away from the river. The road branched east. He continued on it to Seventh Street.

The Seventh Street traffic racket was obnoxious after his quiet months in Ojibwa City and his nights in the woods. He passed restaurants where he and Lily had enjoyed a lot of good food and drink: Molly's Irish Tavern—great Irish whiskey; Seventh Street Tratoria— great pasta; India Palace—great lunch buffet.

None of those were home anymore.

As he walked towards the homeless shelter, he noticed people noticing him. Of course. He was four blocks out of place: what are you doing over here?

The sun had warmed the afternoon almost to the freezing point and he'd pulled up his ski mask. He didn't want anyone looking him in the face. Someone might make a connection. What if he ran into someone who recognized him through his rags because they knew him before or from all the media coverage?

He thought of Hal's tips. Hack began to mutter to himself. But then additional pedestrians were glancing his way.

Solution: up the volume:

"Do you feel lucky?"

"Well, do you, punk?"

"Go ahead—make my day!"

Hal knew his stuff. As Hack passed, every eye was cast up toward the sky or across the street. Couples maintained rigid eye contact with each other. Encouraged, he experimented and turned and twisted his way along the avenue, shouting:

"You talking to me?"

"I don't see anybody else here."

"You talking to me?"

"You talking to me?"

A young well-dressed couple approached holding hands. Hack busted between them. With practiced urban dexterity they parted to let him through and rejoined their hands as they walked on. They never gave a sign they saw him.

He considered hitting someone up for cash. Just for fun—he had plenty. Why not? Anonymity was freedom. No, don't push a good thing too far. Hack reached Sixth Street and sauntered towards the shelter feeling almost cocky.

He passed through the crowd hanging out in front and went into the shelter. He found the cafeteria right away and grabbed a tray from a stack and joined the line. Kind smiling ladies dished out plain lunch time fare: soup, sandwich, chips and peas—even a tuna hot dish with the customary potato chips on top. He loaded his tray and sat down with a bunch of other men at a big table. He didn't know anyone. He didn't say anything. The others all ignored him.

But he did feel right at home.

He finished the meal. Others were dumping the remains of their meals in a big green plastic garbage bin by the exit. He followed their example and dumped his tray and stacked it on the other trays and exited.

The crowd outside was an assortment of races, ages, and genders.

It was the most genuinely diverse crowd Hack had ever seen in St. Paul—certainly more diverse than any Gogol-Chekhov employee meeting.

He saw two grizzled older black guys talking and smoking. The smoke from their cigarettes rose in thin columns straight up into the cold windless air. On an impulse he went over and stood patient and polite waiting for one of them to acknowledge him.

The guy wearing a stocking cap finally looked over at him. "New here?"

"Yes," Hack said.

"We help you?" the other guy asked.

"You got a cigarette? I'll pay."

Stocking Cap reached into his inside coat pocket and pulled out a blue pack. He held it up for Hack to see the few loosies and half-smoked butts poking around in it.

Hack said, "A buck okay?"

Stocking Cap shook his head. "Takes two."

"Deal." Hack dug in his pants pocket and pulled out one loose crumpled bill and four quarters and handed them over.

The man held the pack out. "Pick one."

Hack reached in and pinched one between two fingers and thumb. It was only half a cigarette, but it had a filter. "Thanks."

The two other men waited. Hack said, "You got a light?"

The two men glanced at each other.

"I'll pay for that too," Hack said.

Stocking Cap grinned, showing a few big yellowed teeth separated by big gaps. "Just busting your balls." He took out a pack of matches and handed it to Hack. Hack lit up and handed the matches back.

The two other men waited some more.

Hack got the hint and said, "Thanks," and moved over to stand by the building out of the breeze and smoke his half cigarette. The two men resumed their conversation.

There'd been a time Hack had enjoyed nothing so much as a

cigarette after a meal. Hack hadn't felt that special nicotine stimulation since college—the last time he smoked.

What would Gus say? Or Lily? Unlawful flight to avoid prosecution, breaking and entering, screaming threats at strangers on the street—and now smoking.

And wait'll they hear what I do with that Kabar.

The cigarette was a foul thing. The smoke coated his tongue and mouth with a nasty film. After three rank puffs he tossed it. But fueled by a solid meal and his first nicotine buzz in years he strolled towards the MinneCentre, confident he'd thought of a way to get in.

23 Getting In

The smelly homeless guy disguise—if at this point it was a disguise—was going to give him problems. He needed more than just a way in; he needed freedom to roam once he made it in. He had a plan for that too. It was worth a shot.

Hack knew from experience that before a concert in a big arena there would have to be a sound check and a rehearsal.

Back in his days as a working musician he had played the Centre dozens of times. He walked along the big wall of the huge building to the stage door. He stationed himself on the sidewalk about thirty feet away.

Hack stamped and jumped around to keep warm for about forty bitter minutes. A big black limousine pulled up to the curb across the side walk in front of the stage door. A woman in her late thirties got out through the curb side back passenger door. Two men and another woman emerged after her.

Hack recognized the second woman. It was the folk singer Fredra Colo. She was slender and slightly above average in height with long blond hair parted in the middle. She carried an acoustic guitar case in her left hand. She looked around at the Minnesota winter with obvious distaste. With her right hand, she pulled her thin jacket close, trying to hold on to the warmth she'd enjoyed in the limo.

Fredra was a one-name performer famous in a musical world Hack seldom paid attention to. He knew she wrote and sang a lot of sensitive songs about being a girl turning into a woman and about global warming and about social injustice, but he'd never paid much attention to her or her songs.

One of Hack's college girlfriends—what was her name?—had played some of Fredra's songs for him, but he didn't relate to the experiences in the lyrics and the music seemed unchallenging—a far cry from Mozart or Thelonious Monk or even the Eagles. But Hack also remembered what a music snob he'd been at that age.

The other three all carried instrument cases. They must be her sidemen: one woman guitar player, one crew cut male bass player and a dark bearded man carrying a cymbal case—the drummer.

The drummer shook his head. "This is Hell. We're in Hell."

The bass player exhaled and watched the vapor in the air. "I can see my breath!"

The drummer said, "That's just a lifetime of trapped cigarette smoke making a break for freedom."

"No, dammit. That's water vapor."

"When did you breathe healthy air in or out after ninth grade?"

The woman guitarist spoke: "Can it, will you? We'll do the gig, catch the red-eye and wake up warm back in L.A. tomorrow morning."

The Stage Door opened out. Lily stood in the entrance holding the door open. "Fredra, I'm so excited to meet you."

And Hack was excited to see Lily—dammit.

Lily added, "Thanks so much for coming. It will mean so much to our entire community."

Fredra smiled and stepped towards Lily and offered her hand. "It's an honor. And you are?"

Lily smiled back. "Lily Lapidos."

The two smiling women shook hands and turned and went into the arena. The side players followed. The limousine took off.

Hack stomped and hopped around some more. A few more people drifted by and showed their passes and entered.

Another twenty minutes passed before Hack saw a musician he recognized—Rocky Shores. Rocky was a black pianist and keyboard player who'd been part of the Minnesota music scene as long as any living musician could remember. Hack hadn't seen him for at least ten years. Rocky now walked with the very stiff and deliberate gait of an old man. He carried a brown cardboard satchel by two flimsy rectangular handles. He walked right past Hack.

Hack said, "Rocky."

Rocky stopped and turned and peered at him through thick glasses. "Do I know you?"

Hack took the gamble. "It's me. Nat Wilder."

"Oh yeah. Of course. What are you all dressed down for?"

"A gag I want to play on some friends."

"It'll work."

"Counting on it. You're here to play the concert, right?"

"Yeah. They bring their own band but they need someone on keyboards for glue and filler and the like. A quick read. Which they know I am."

"That's you."

"And you too, as I recall."

"Yeah. Me too."

Rocky stood stoic and patient. He gave no sign he was aware of Hack's circumstance. "So how you been all these years?"

"Making out. Although I've been having some ups and downs lately."

"Fun running into you. Got to go. Sound check and rehearsal." Rocky turned to head for the stage door.

"Say, Rocky. How much they paying you?"

Rocky stopped and swiveled his head slowly. "Damn fine for one night for what I got to do, which won't be much. Five hundred dollars."

"That is good."

"Damn fine. But peanuts compared to what the big act—what's her name—is getting."

"Well, suppose I give you six hundred and take your place."

Rocky stared through his goggles.

"Okay, so let's say seven hundred?"

"Now why would you do that?"

"I'm a big Fredra fan. If I show her what I can do maybe I make a connection. Who knows? She might want me for a tour or something. Big paydays for that."

"Well, you know, I'm a professional. Never missed a gig. I haven't kept working steady and supported my family and put four kids through college all these years by failing my obligations."

"You know I can play anything they come up with. And you

don't tour these days, do you?"

"Naw. Way past that. They don't even let me drive any more. My grandson had to drop me here."

"How about eight hundred?"

Hack saw the calculation going on behind Rocky's thick lenses. "How about a thousand?"

"Fair enough. Hang on." Hack stepped close to the wall and turned his back to shield his body from the eyes of the world. He dug the Gus cash clip out of his pocket. He separated out ten one-hundred-dollar bills, stuck the clip and remaining cash back in his pocket and turned and handed the bills to Rocky.

"Nice." Rocky took the bills and handed Hack the brown satchel. "Here's some charts they sent me. It'll take a pro like you ten minutes to learn them cold."

"Got it."

"And you know the drill. They sent me this badge. You got to wear it to get in and around." Rocky handed Hack the badge and thick plastic string it hung on.

Hack took the badge and hung it by its string around his neck. "Got that too." He headed for the stage door.

"Nat!"

Hack stopped.

Rocky said, "Be very very careful in there."

"I plan to be."

"Good. You know, I always liked you a lot. And those under-rehearsed gigs can be lethal."

"I know."

"Don't find out for real."

Hack watched as Rocky turned and trudged away, pulling out his cell phone and punching in a number.

Hack strode to the stage door. He waved his badge with a friendly grin and a big show of confidence. The security guy wrinkled his face as he gave Hack a once over through the glass door, but then shrugged and pressed a button. After all, Hack wore the badge.

The door opened out and Hack stepped through it into the MinneCentre.

24 Rock The Unity!

Hack stood looking up and down a back hall of the MinneCentre. For the first time in years he felt a once-familiar rush. A new gig. New music to play. New people to play with. He admitted to himself he was sort of exhilarated at the thought.

And nervous too—and not about the cops catching him, but about the gig. What if he flubbed something in front of thousands of people? Well, wouldn't be the first time. He reminded himself the music was not his priority.

Nevertheless.

As a working musician his first few years right after college, Hack had entered the Centre through this same stage door dozens of times.

As he oriented himself, memories of the Centre's inner geography drifted back. Dressing rooms and locker rooms were located on a lower level down those metal stairs on his left.

He recalled that one of the many facilities in the vast complex was a small two-hundred seat theater. He had played there as music director for some long-ago stage production. The theater had its own dressing room. He descended one flight of stairs and made one right turn and then another. He went down another flight and took a left to the dressing room.

Everything looked the way he remembered. Costumes for the current production hung on small racks with paper labels for the names of actors.

There was a bathroom with a small shower and fresh towels hanging on a rack just outside.

No one around. Hack took off his filthy rags and laid then on the floor. He scrubbed himself clean in his first hot shower since—was it six days ago?—and stepped out and toweled himself off. Naked except for the towel, he inspected the clothing racks.

From the wardrobe the play looked to be set in the 1930's.

A clipboard hung on the wall with a sign-in sheet and a pen hanging on it by a string. The sheet listed shows Thursday through Saturday—no show tonight, which was very good.

The top of the sheet read "Call List For 'Of Mice and Men'." Below that in big bold letter: "REQUIREMENT: SIGN IN FOR EVERY PERFORMANCE." Only a few scrawls littered the sheet. One signature read "Bugs Bunny." It was obvious the requirement was more honored in the breach than in the observance.

Hack knew the story of the play. He inspected the clothing rack again, searching for George's costume. He doubted a costume for the giant Lennie character would fit him.

Of course, no underwear provided. Actors were expected to bring their own. He had none he cared to wear ever again. Much as he hated the feeling, he'd have to go natural.

He found George's pants, a belt, socks, shoes, a dress shirt and a jacket. He put them all on. He transferred everything from the pockets of his previous outfit to his new one, this time meticulous not to leave behind a single item. George's clothes hung too large on him, but that was an advantage. The suit jacket draped long over his left side, shielding from view the six-inch Kabar and sheath he stuck sideways in his belt. He had smuggled it inside Rocky's music case.

He spotted an electric shaver and used it and checked himself in the mirror. Completely clean-shaven for the first time in years. As Hal would say, excellent.

On top of a high rack he saw a stack of thirties-style fedoras and homburgs. He picked out the fedora with the highest dome and the widest brim and put it on. Again too large, but again an advantage.

He checked the mirror again. Much better. If he just kept his head pointed down at the keyboard he might get away with it.

He picked Hal's dirty clothes off the floor and searched for a place to dump them. He found an aluminum garbage can in a dim reach of the hallway and dumped Hal's clothes there.

Hack paused. A touch of sorrow brushed him. His goodbye to Hal's clothes was a goodbye to Hal. Hack glanced around the empty dark corridor. No one around. He felt a powerful urge to articulate some kind of ceremonial recognition. He spoke it out loud. "So long, friend."

Hack's voice seemed to echo in the hallway.

Then he picked up Rocky's cardboard satchel and walked down the hall to the stairs and up to the big arena.

25 Listen While You Work

For a while Hack was lost in a labyrinth looking for the Arena Stage. Twice he took wrong turns. Finally, he spotted a big sign with an arrow pointing towards a door: "Auditorium." He followed the arrow and passed through the door and then huge hanging curtains and found himself on a stage at least forty by twenty feet.

Techs scurried around laying cables. Other techs followed behind and taped the cables to the floor so no one would trip. Stage monitor speakers and microphone stands stood scattered all about.

Stage right was a big black beautiful Steinway grand piano and behind that a triple bank of electronic keyboards one above the other. A round black stool sat between the instruments. He'd be able to swivel and play whatever instrument he was called on to play.

Clusters of people stood talking near the center of the stage. One group included Fredra. Tariq Daghestani was chatting with Fredra and her band mates. They were all smiling and nodding.

Hack took a deep breath and headed for the piano stool.

The woman guitar player spotted him. She was a thin woman with short brown hair, taller than Hack. She wore a long green shift. She came over. "Are you Rocky?"

He held up Rocky's cardboard satchel. "I am."

Concerned: "I thought you were black."

"So did I."

"Is that a joke?"

"Feels like one sometimes."

She narrowed her eyes. "There are some rules you should know."

"Okay."

"First, Fredra's got her own band and we all know all the songs. I'm the Music Director."

"Pleasure to meet you."

"Is having a woman Music Director an issue for you?"

He shrugged.

"You read through the music we overnighted, right?"

"Of course," Hack lied like every hired musician since Pharaoh's Egypt.

"You're just here for the occasional piano riff so the songs sound like Fredra's fans expect from the recordings. And the sweetener—eggs. Use the keyboard string voices, of course. You listened to the recordings too, right?"

"Right." Eggs were whole notes—long sweet chords from the electronic keyboards to add a lush background.

"Nothing fancy. You're not here to show everyone what a virtuoso you are."

Hack was here for reasons that had nothing to do with Fredra or her songs. Which meant he couldn't afford to get fired. Just grin and bear it. He grinned. "Got it."

She said, "I don't want you to think I'm a bitch."

"The thought never crossed my mind."

A suspicious expression: "But I don't actually care if you do. Sometimes we've had that problem with local musicians. So I need to lay down the rules ahead of time. I'm just being fair."

"Fair."

"Now, there's one other thing. An important thing. A very important thing. The Most Important Thing."

"Sounds important."

She plugged on. "Normally we tell the local musicians in writing ahead of time as part of the contract they have to sign to get the gig. But this event came up too sudden."

She leaned forward to impart The Most Important Thing.

Hack waited.

"No Eye Contact."

"Beg your pardon?"

"No eye contact. With Fredra. You're not to make any eye contact with Fredra at any time before or during or after the entire performance. None. Just do your job and take off. I'll pay you afterwards."

"Even when she's singing?"

"Especially when she's singing. She's an iconic figure. She has major social and personal issues on her mind. The world can't afford to have some keyboard guy distract her."

"I see."

She crossed her thin arms in front of her. "Any questions?"

He had to ask the question his experience insisted on. "What if I need some feedback about what's going on? You know, if something unexpected happens?"

"That's what rehearsals are for."

"Sometimes things happen you don't rehearse. You know, something spontaneous."

"We don't do spontaneous. Understand?"

"I understand."

"You make any eye contact with anyone it's with me. Then if I decide it's an appropriate eye contact, I pass the eye contact further up the line to Fredra. If there is any. Which there shouldn't be."

"Okay."

"I'm the Music Director and I'm the designated eye contact person."

"You're designated."

"I make all eye contact. Got it?"

Hack nodded. "Got it."

"And I don't mean to be a bitch about it, but that's the way it is."

First he'd grinned, now he bore it. Hang on to the gig. That's what's important here.

She eyed him one more time, then, possibly a bit mollified, she stalked back to her group. He saw her say something to the bass player and point to Hack. The bass player shrugged. She caught something Fredra said and turned to join the group laughter. The bass player glanced over at Hack and rolled his eyes.

She hadn't even told Hack her name.

Hack walked over to the piano and sat down on the stool behind it. He ran his fingers lightly over the entire range of keys from right to left and then back again from left to right. He liked to do that with a new piano. He felt somehow it helped his touch. Or maybe it was just a superstition.

He swiveled the stool and checked out the keyboard rack to his right. The rack held three keyboards one above the other: a Roland, a Yamaha and a Kurzweil. Good. Nothing too recent; he knew all three and which buttons to press for which sounds. He opened up Rocky's satchel and took out the sheet music and laid it on the rack above the Steinway's keys to inspect.

An older man with a graying blond beard popped up to the right of the piano like a genie out of a bottle. He stuck out his hand. "Johnson."

"Rocky."

They shook hands.

"I'm here to tune it up."

"Go to it." Hack stepped away for the twenty minutes it took Johnson to tune the piano.

The sound check lasted about an hour. They tested all the instruments and microphones through all the monitors. Everything ran smooth. The techs knew their job. Everyone took a break before rehearsing Fredra's songs.

Hack took advantage of the break to stand and read through the sheet music. Daghestani was standing alone to the immediate right of the piano. In the relative quiet, Hack heard the mild thump of footsteps echoing behind him on the hollow stage floor. He glanced over and recognized Amalki and Khaled.

By reflex Hack pulled his big hat farther down over his face. But what for? As far as Hack knew, Daghestani couldn't recognize him and neither of the two killers had ever gotten a good look at him in a good light. Or clean-shaven. Plus they thought they'd already killed him.

The three men were talking in voices too low for Hack to hear. But they were so close. Should he risk it?

Hack sauntered around to where the three men stood. "Excuse me, gentlemen," he said. "There might be a problem with the piano action. Got to take a peek under the hood."

Daghestani gave him a regal smile and a small courtly bow and backed up a few feet. Khaled turned without expression to face Daghestani in his new location. Amalki shook his head in apparent irritation and turned likewise to face Daghestani. Covering Amalki's left ear was a new heavy bandage of thick gauze pads and surgical tape.

"Wow," Hack said. "What's up with your ear? Traffic accident?"

Amalki didn't turn his head. "Yes."

"Woman driver?"

Amalki still didn't turn. He snapped, "Not your business." But his two accomplices shared a glance of knowing amusement.

"Sorry." Hack lifted the piano lid high. To hold it in place he raised the top board prop and stuck it into its cup on the underside of the lid. He leaned over and down as if to inspect the hammers and strings. He was surprised to observe the steadiness of his right hand as he plucked a few strings for credibility. Was he adjusting to his new way of life?

He pretended to poke and snoop among the hammers and strings, also trying not to interfere with his ability to hear the three men.

The men spoke low and in accented English. Hack caught only random snatches:

"Khaybar…"

"Tonight and again tomorrow…"

"Exactly…two in a row…maximum impact…"

"Lennie…"

"Abadi's mess…"

"True. Abadi…Amir…Wilder."

"Khaybar…"

"And the woman?"

Loudest of all, a harsh croak from Amalki: "Never mind the woman!"

Hack was still leaning under the propped-up lid pretending to inspect the sound board when the men stopped talking. He caught an evocative familiar scent—her favorite perfume. He glanced back below his arm and saw the fourth set of legs as she approached.

Lily.

Great.

Hack heard Lily ask, "Tariq, is there anything else you're going to need?"

"Not at all. You are one truly amazing woman. Getting Fredra to sing is a wonderful coup—a feather in your cap. By the way, Lily, have you met my colleague Tayeb Chahuan?"

"Not yet. It's a pleasure."

"And this is my student, Khaled. Brilliant and original."

"Pleased to meet you as well."

So Amalki's real name was Tayeb Chahuan. Or the other way around.

"I am pleased as well," Amalki/Chahuan said. "Must be off. Things to take care of."

"I too," added Khaled. "Obligations to our community never end."

Hack heard their footsteps on the stage floor as they walked away.

Bent over as it was, Hack's back began to nag at him. Plus he was feeling more and more ridiculous. How long could he pretend to fiddle with these strings?"

Evidently Daghestani was asking himself the same question. "Say Rocky—that's your name, if I heard right?"

"Uhm mmh."

"Everything okay in there?"

"Uhm mmh."

"I didn't realize there was so much to playing the piano. I suppose it was naive, but I thought you guys just sat down and played."

"Oh no," Lily said. "There's a lot more to it than that. My ex-husband is—was—is a pianist." She paused. "Sorry. I mean—let's not talk about him tonight of all nights."

"Let's not," Daghestani agreed.

"These last few nights I lie awake and wonder."

"Which of us really knows his brother? Or her husband? You've done nothing wrong. And if even if you had—which you haven't—all you have given tonight and are continuing to give for our communities and our shared values will continue to compensate."

Hack repressed a cough that might damage his back.

"Yes..." Daghestani said, apparently to Lily.

"Yes..." Lily responded.

Hack grunted, "Um," but no one seemed to hear.

Daghestani said, "You will surely see. This night and its beauty will wipe out all painful memories. And there is a future."

"It will be a night to remember," Lily said.

"Yes, it will." Daghestani said. "For everyone."

"We'll talk later," she said.

"I hope so."

Lily's footsteps receded. Hack gave it a long moment and then straightened up and stuck his right hand against his lower back and stretched his left up and then behind his neck. He grinned at Daghestani. "All good. Ready to play."

Daghestani clapped Hack's upper left arm with a surprisingly powerful grip. "Wonderful. We are so grateful for your invaluable contribution. And thank you ahead of time for all you will do tonight."

"It's a thrill for me too." Daghestani released Hack's arm and Hack walked back to his stool, stretching as he went.

The band gathered on stage again and they ran all the Fredra songs, which weren't as syrupy as Hack had feared. Throughout the rehearsal, Hack made a point of avoiding eye contact, not only with Fredra but with everyone else. He had enjoyed his escapade with the terrorists but he knew he'd been stupid. He vowed to himself to keep his empty hatted head down and his eyes on the keys the rest of the night.

At rehearsal's end Music Director Woman clicked off her amp. Then with care she set down her guitar and leaned it against the amp.

She clapped her hands and announced, "OK. Good job, people." She shot Hack a glance and gave the briefest nod as if to say, even you.

She continued, "Enjoy your meals. Be back ready to play at 8:30 P.M. sharp. We perform at nine."

It was about five P.M.. Three and one-half hours to kill.

Hack stood and wandered off stage through the curtains and then through a side door. He found himself in a long hallway. He strolled down it until he found a bench. No one was around. He sat down to puzzle over what he had overheard from the three men.

It didn't sound good. Something tonight and something tomorrow night as well? He'd definitely heard the word "Khaybar." Had he also heard the word "Lennie?" If so, how did that fit in?

A few minutes later, he was still pondering when he recognized Sarai's sweet flute-like voice. Sam Lapidos and Sarai were walking hand in hand down the corridor in Hack's direction. Sam held his granddaughter's hand while she piped away about Tu BiShvat.

Hack pried his eyes off his daughter and took a cell phone from his pocket and faced down and pretended to key it.

The two passed by. Hack glanced sideways down the hall after them and saw Lily coming from the other direction. The three stopped about twenty-five yards away and talked. Hack couldn't hear what they said.

Lily took Sarai's hand. Sam bent down to kiss Sarai's cheek. Sarai kissed him back. Then Sam kissed Lily and Lily gave Sam a stiff hug and a perfunctory kiss on the cheek. Over Sam's shoulder Hack saw the sour expression on Lily's face. Lily turned and led Sarai away.

Sarai happened to glance back and her eyes met Hack's and widened. She swiveled her head straight ahead like a robot. Sam watched Lily and Sarai disappear around a corner down the hall. Then Sam turned and strolled back in Hack's direction.

Hack kept his head pointed down at the phone. He saw Sam's legs stop on the floor in front of him. Sam's suit pants were a classy blue serge. Sam always wore custom tailored suits and silk shirts and ties and

Italy's priciest shoes.

In his practice, Sam represented not only the most powerful rich but the most destitute poor. He said he wanted even his poorest clients to appear to juries like they deserved and could afford the most expensive lawyers. Hack also suspected a measure of vanity.

Today Sam's shoes were Testoni Norvogese, fifteen hundred dollars a pop and polished to an ebony glow.

Sam sat down on the bench next to Hack. He was a wiry man, half bald, with a weathered olive-skinned raptor face. Hack heard Sam say, "Your phone's off."

Hack said nothing. He just waited, hoping the man would go away.

Sam said, "You one of the musicians tonight?"

Hack snuck the briefest sideways glance. Sam was staring straight ahead at the wall on the other side of the hall. "Yes. How'd you know?"

"Came early to watch the rehearsal. Thought my granddaughter would enjoy it."

"Nice thought."

"Funny. My former son-in-law's also a musician."

"Really?"

"You play piano, right?"

"Yes."

"Funny. My former son-in-law plays the piano."

Hack waited for Sam to ask, "You a hunted fugitive accused of two murders? Funny…"

But Sam didn't. Instead: "I'm a lawyer myself."

Hack had no choice, so he followed along. "Really."

"Got a tough case. My client is my former son-in-law's best friend. He's in jail and the feds won't let him go."

"Really."

"Having a hell of a time getting the legally required discovery from the prosecutors. They're supposed to explain the charges and show me the evidence but they stonewall. Or they got prostate issues and they piss the information out one meaningless drop a time."

"Really."

"They're like octopuses. They spew a cloud of ink about "national security" and "sources and methods" they can't reveal. They've got the judge almost buffaloed so far. But I'll keep working him. I know him; if he figures out the feds are lying to him he'll come down hard. But for now no real discovery and no bail. My former son-in-law's best friend is really up against it."

"What's he say? I mean, your former son-in-law's best friend?"

"Can't tell you. Privileged. But I can tell you I'm really ticked."

"Really."

"Really. You know, my former son-in-law's a piano player like you, but I don't recall his vocabulary being quite so limited. You got nothing to say but 'really'?"

Hack glanced over again. Sam was keeping his gaze on the opposite wall.

Sam said, "Don't you piano players stick together? Maybe you can fill in for my former son-in-law like you're filling in for Rocky."

Okay, so Sam knew he wasn't Rocky. Sam was a big jazz fan and would know that even if he hadn't recognized Hack, which obviously he had. "Does the word 'Khaybar' mean anything to you?"

"Khaybar?" Sam stiffened as if someone had stuck a steel rod up his back end. "Yes. I know that word."

"You know what it means?"

"I know exactly what it means. What it means historically and what it means now. I know who says it and why."

"Who says it?"

"Jihadis. Islamists who want to kill Jews. Jews like me and like my former son-in-law's ex-wife and his daughter. What about it?"

"Something's going down that has to do with Khaybar."

"Something. What exactly?"

"Don't know. But something really bad."

"That's always the case with Khaybar. Anything more?"

"And…" Hack might as well say it. "Toe Lip."

"Toe Lip?" Now Sam finally turned to face Hack. "What the Hell is Toe Lip?"

Hack shrugged.

Sam went back to looking at his wall. "And where does a lawyer go to learn more about this Khaybar and Toe Lip stuff?"

Now Hack regretted even more losing both his basement Khaybar computer and the flash drive backup. "On some documents. Which I hope still exist. On a laptop."

"Which is where?"

"Your client's son."

Sam sighed as long and as deep a sigh as Hack had ever heard. It seemed to shake the man's thin frame. "My client? We're talking about Augustus Albert Dropo?"

"Sure."

"Gus has a son? That shithead."

"Gus didn't tell you he has a son?" In other circumstances, Hack would have laughed. Instead he just shook his head. "That Gus."

"That shithead," Sam insisted. "And this son—"

"Little Gus—actually he prefers 'LG'—about fifteen years old—

"

"Has a laptop with documents—"

"Documents in Arabic that talk about Khaybar and about Toe Lip."

"In Arabic. You—I mean—piano players learn Arabic in piano playing school?"

"No." Hack explained about the Arabic translation site.

"So 'Toe Lip' is probably a bad translation of something else."

"Seems likely."

"And where is this miniature Gus?"

"If you can find him, he's probably hiding out by their house nearby in the woods. But forget about finding him if he doesn't want you to."

"Like his father? What the world needs—another Gus. And that's why they call him 'Little Gus'?"

"You get things quick."

"That's my job. How would I convince this little LG fellow to want to be found?"

"You can't."

"Don't be too sure. Convincing people is my line."

Hack made his decision. "There is one possibility. But you'll be risking your Testoni Norvogese shoes." And he told Sam about the shack.

Sam jumped up and handed Hack a card. "My number. In case something else comes up about my client." Before Hack could say another word, Sam scurried down the hall, hard dress shoe heels clicking on the tiles.

Dammit! Sam hadn't given Hack the chance to tell him about the *Mein Kampf* book or about the three-way conversation Hack had overheard onstage. And Hack was sure he'd heard the word "Khaybar" onstage too.

But one of the three had also said the word "Lennie." Hack got up and walked in the opposite direction to the stairway and then down it.

In a few minutes he was back in the "Of Mice and Men" dressing room. It was probably ridiculous. Paranoid, too. Stupid, even. But it wasn't far-fetched to imagine people who went around beheading other people might also plant a bomb.

26 The Dating Game

Hack searched the dressing room top to bottom and left to right and found nothing of interest. Then he searched it again. A bomb? He didn't know what a bomb looked like. A clock? A black bowling ball like in the old cartoons?

The word "Lennie" he'd overheard argued for a closer look at the Lennie costume. Bib overalls. A denim jacket. An old style billed cap like Lenin or Lennon wore. A yellow paper tag taped to the jacket read "Jack Henderson." The garments were light. For sure no bomb.

He thought, maybe I should get off this and figure out a way to get Amalki or Khaled alone.

Hack ran his hands over the Lennie overalls and felt a slight thickening in the right front pocket. He found and removed a single neatly folded sheet of paper and unfolded it. It was a flier with a large print bold face heading, black letters on yellow:

ROCK THE UNITY IS A CONCERT FOR HATE
Don't Let It Happen!

Below was a screed about "Muzzies" and the threat its author declared they posed to western civilization and the white race.

Jack Henderson—the actor who played Lennie—was into some anti-Muslim hate group? In Hack's experience, actors were like musicians and generally considered themselves leftists or progressives or radicals—leaning more towards irrational love than irrational hate. But like everything else in Hack's current world, it was possible.

The flier in the pocket was the only noteworthy item Hack found in the entire dressing room. He broadened his search to the two other dressing rooms. Nothing interesting. He wandered the dark hallway searching. Time was running out. A clock on the wall read 7:30 P.M..

Closing in on his 8:30 call to upstairs to play.

He found himself by the trash can where he'd dumped Hal's clothes. He overcame the aversion he felt to disturbing Hal's things and sorted through them anyway. Beneath the garments he found discarded yogurt lids and paper coffee cups sprinkled with coffee grounds, as well as dead apple cores and fruit rinds—no greasy burger wrappings or sticky cupcake wrappers for this health-minded crew. Mingled in were some soggy scraps of paper. He picked up one of the scraps. Another hate flier. He lifted Hal's clothes out of the can and grabbed more scraps. More hate.

With both hands he grabbed the can by its top and tilted it over to dump its entire contents across the floor. Mingled with the soft spattering and sloshing he heard a hard clatter of metal. Something small and black bounced on the floor—a cell phone.

He picked it up. It was on. Odd. Why would someone discard a cell phone? Especially a phone left on?

Hack considered. He'd read that a cell phone could trigger a bomb. But this cell phone had no attached cables or wires.

Too simple. Hack had programmed phones for the browser PrivaNation he'd written at GC. A phone was just another computer. Someone could program a phone so that a call or a text to one phone could trigger a call or a text to another phone, which in turn could trigger another. Phones could form links in a chain that might ultimately lead to a bomb.

A second garbage can sat in the farthest end of the dark hall. As Hack came near he caught a distinctive petrochemical stink. An accelerant? He dumped the second can's contents onto the floor—rags soaked in something like cigarette lighter fluid or barbecue starter fluid, more fliers, and another cell phone. He picked up the phone—also on. And someone had stuck some kind of shiny silvery metal to its side.

He inspected the silvery metal. Too soft for aluminum. Magnesium? Hack felt around the phone and noticed a fine crack in the case. Hack took the Swiss Army Knife out of his pocket and pried the case apart. Someone had spanned the gap between the battery's plus and minus connectors with the shiny metal. To cause a short circuit?

A short circuit could cause a spark that heated the magnesium—assuming that's what it was—to ignition and then the magnesium could fire the accelerant-soaked contents of the bin.

What about the fire sensors? There—on the ceiling. One hung directly over the bin. Hack didn't have a ladder, but he didn't need one. He could see from where he stood that someone had taken a hammer to the nozzle. No fire suppressor liquid.

Arson.

Just in case, he turned off the phone with the magnesium. He stomped it repeatedly with his heel until it cracked into pieces.

He inspected the first phone. He turned it over and started running through its settings. No previous call or text history. Unlike the second, physically it seemed completely normal. Nothing unusual about it all.

Suddenly it buzzed in his hand. A text.

Just one word: "Khaybar."

Had he prevented a fire? He thought so. But it seemed a shoddy operation. Easily set up but just as easily stymied by a random non-expert like Hack.

Was this the best they could do?

He scooped the fragments of the second phone up from the floor and dropped them into his jacket's left pocket.

The time on the first phone read 8:10. He could still make the gig. Didn't want to put Rocky on the spot.

The text came from an unblocked number. Someone was leaving a trail. Shoddy again. He dialed the number and held the phone to his ear. It rang at the other end.

No answer.

Hack dialed again.

Still no answer.

He dialed again.

A tentative "Hello?" Hack knew the voice.

"Hi there, Amalki. Or is it Tayeb?"

"Who is this?"

"You don't recognize me? We've met twice."

"When was that?"

"When you killed me in Ojibwa City. You killed so many guys you don't remember me in particular?"

"That's crazy talk. I don't know who you are or what you're talking about."

"Of course not. But you do have a problem."

"I have no problem. You have the problem. I don't know who you are or what you're talking about or why you're calling me."

"You screwed up. And I'm taking a wild guess your boss doesn't suffer screw ups."

Silence. Had Hack hit a nerve? "Is that what happened to your pal Ahmed Abadi? Did he screw up and wind up headless in a ditch? I know I didn't kill him."

"This is your best?"

Hack plowed ahead. "The best is yet to come. I'm giving you a special one-time-only offer. Meet me in Ojibwa City and you receive at no extra cost one free chance to clean up your big booboo. That's more than fair, don't you think?"

Now Amalki seemed yet more confident. "You really are crazy. Whoever you are. And of course I've never been to this city you're talking about and I won't be going there—wherever it is."

"Then you probably don't know or care about the intersection where Highway 15 meets Childress Avenue. And you've certainly got no reason to show up there tonight at one A.M.."

"Exactly."

"So I'll give you a reason. I'm Wilder—the guy you promised your very demanding boss Daghestani you already killed. I'm in the MinneCenter basement, where I just put the kibosh on your arson fire you promised him you'd start. Face me or face him, Tayeb? or Amalki?—by the way, what do you need two names for? You'll be dead by tomorrow morning anyway." Hack clicked off.

8:20. Could still make the gig. But time for one more phone call. He took out the business card Sam had given him and used Amalki's phone again.

Sam answered on the first ring.

"Hi, I don't know if you remember me, but I'm Rocky. The piano player. We met and chatted in the hall a little while ago."

"Yes, I remember. How can I help?"

"You can check something out. Or have Security do it. I was freshening up for tonight's performance in a downstairs dressing room. The one for "Of Mice and Men." There's a strange smell in the hall near there. Like someone spilled lighter fluid or something like that. Very strong. Might be a fire hazard. It's probably nothing, but you know, with all the stuff going on in the news, I thought I'd let someone know and I thought of you."

"Much appreciated."

"No problem." Hack turned off the phone and stuck it in his pocket with the pieces of the smashed phone. He dashed back to the stairs and then up towards the stage.

27 Ear Boy

The concert was easy and fun. Fredra sang and the crowd swayed and held hands and sang along. Every so often Hack chimed in from the keyboards with his glue and his eggs. He felt about as indispensable as the triangle player in the Minnesota Symphony.

Music Director Woman often stepped to the microphone to share some private joke or snarky political jibe with Fredra and by extension with the crowd. Hack wondered if her jokes were a strategy to establish her intimate relationship with the star. From her jibes he could sum up her outlook as a single primal political principle: us good, them bad. Her presumed consensus was everyone had come because they were with the good. No one dissented, although it seemed to Hack a lot of the audience sat on their hands when she spoke.

Fredra never said a word about politics. She just sang.

The concert ran to 10:45 P.M., later than Hack had hoped, given his date with Amalki. It was clear Fredra enjoyed the adulation and was reluctant to stop. But even before the finale, people started drifting away and the crowd began to thin out.

The concert wound down and Fredra took her bows. The instant she left the stage techs stormed it and began winding up cables and disconnecting microphones and rolling amps off to wherever amps went. Hack left the sheet music on the keyboard. Music Director woman walked over and handed him a check without a word. Hack figured he would mail it to Rocky the next chance he had. Maybe from jail.

Before heading off for his date with Amalki, Hack took a few minutes to use the bathroom one time in case he didn't get a chance later—another thing his dad had advised him to do.

As Hack walked down a corridor towards the stage door he saw he was going to pass Music Director Woman and Fredra. Music Director woman glared at him.

Definitely the moment for Eye Contact. Hack looked directly into Fredra's eyes and beamed her his brightest smile. She smiled back and mouthed the words "Great job! Thanks!" and blew him a sisterly kiss.

As Hack passed on through the door he pictured Music Director Woman's eyes as two lasers crisping the skin of his neck.

He thought, Maybe LG's right. I am goofing around a lot more the past few days.

He took a left down the corridor and there stood Lily about thirty yards away. She was part of a group waiting for an elevator. Sarai stood next to her fiddling with a small electronic game device. Amalki had positioned himself in front of Lily, apparently chatting her up. He dwarfed her. He was grinning down at her round olive skinned face and she was listening to him with what looked like rapt attention.

Hack spotted a small alcove with a water fountain. He ducked into the space and peered around the corner towards Lily and Sarai and Amalki.

He took Amalki's cell phone out of his pocket and clicked it on and dialed Lily. He watched her reach into her purse and pull out her phone. "Yes?"

"Whatever you do, don't get on any elevator with that guy."

"Nat. Are you crazy?" He saw her step away and separate herself from Amalki and the group. She signaled with raised index finger for Amalki and the others to wait a moment while she took the call. She turned her back on the group and took three steps away and huddled over her phone.

Hack spoke low. "You're crazy if you go anywhere or take Sarai anywhere with that guy. Don't you wonder how he got that ear?"

"Where are you?" She glanced around. "Can you see me?"

"I can see you're both in big danger with that guy."

"Nat, please turn yourself in."

"You think I killed those people?"

No answer.

"Answer me. You think I killed those people?"

"I can't say until I see all the evidence."

"That's one Hell of a thing to say to someone you lived with ten years."

"You lied about losing your job, didn't you? You claimed you quit and you never told me they fired you."

"You can't compare losing a job to killing people. I didn't kill anyone."

"I know you've been calling Sarai every day. Behind my back. And you can compare lying to lying. Are you lying now?"

A bigger anger flared up. "I heard you talking to those guys— Daghestani and Khaled and Amalki."

"Amalki? Who's that?"

"All right—Tayeb or whatever his name is today. The point is people call me murderer and you don't stick up for me. A serial murderer even."

"Nat, you need help. Turn yourself in. It's the only sane thing to do. I'll see you get help. I'll stick by you."

"You didn't stick by me even three hours ago. What kind of ex-wife are you, anyway?"

"This is not the time or place for hashing out post-marital differences. Just turn yourself in."

"Talk to Sam."

"What?"

"Talk to Sam. And in the meantime don't get on any elevator with what's-his-name and don't go anywhere alone with him and whatever you do don't let him anywhere near my daughter."

Hack peeked around his corner again and saw Lily shrugging to Amalki to show apology. She signaled to him with her index finger: just one minute more. By now the crowd in front of the elevator had thinned. Sarai was still focused on her game device, but she glanced up and apparently by accident once again looked directly into Hack's eyes. She shook her head hard once and looked down at her game.

Lily deployed her all-too-familiar instructional voice, dripping out one distinctly enunciated syllable after another: "I will go anywhere I want with whomever I want and whenever I want." Then, anticlimactically: "To go, I mean."

Hack forced calm into his own voice. "Please talk to Sam. And no elevators."

Hack reached his finger down to cut the call.

Just before his finger hit the button, he heard, "What was that you said about his ear?"

28 Feeding the Hungry

Hack stepped out through the Stage Door onto the sidewalk. A slight layer of new snow dusted the pavement. To shield against the bitter air, he pulled his light stolen jacket close. He estimated the temperature as about twenty degrees. The snow seemed to have stopped and visibility was decent. He should be able to reach the Fox and make his date with Amalki in time.

He walked the mile back to his Fox without incident. The ninety-minute drive to Ojibwa City was uneventful. He passed a police car going the other way but it seemed to pay him no mind. At twelve thirty he pulled to a stop and parked on Childress Avenue about one hundred yards past County 15.

He got out of the car and dug his backpack out of the trunk and brought it into the back seat of the warm passenger compartment. The space was cramped, but he managed with only a few contortions to change out of his George costume into his winter gear. Then he got out again and put on his skis and watched the highway and waited.

Nothing happened. Only an occasional car or truck whizzed by on Highway 15. No one at all came up or down Childress.

He checked the clock inside the Fox. One fifteen. Then one thirty. Then two A.M.. Nothing.

Amalki had stood him up.

What now?

Hack had chosen this spot to park for a reason. It was relatively close by ski to his new favorite camp site.

He'd spend the night in the wilderness and come up with something else in the morning.

The snow pack looked good. He estimated his travel time at two and one-half hours at most.

His estimate was off. It took him about three hours.

This time Hack spotted the colorful wrappers in the tree right away. He pulled up and stripped off his skis and boots and prepared for a comfortable night in his warm cozy log.

A new noise caught his attention. The familiar piercing whine rose and fell in intensity and pitch as it blasted its way across the snow towards him—a snowmobile.

Like a lot of cross-country skiers, Hack hated snowmobiles. The big treads chewed up the trails the Department of Natural Resources groomed for hobby skiers. Snowmobilers routinely ignored the "No snowmobiles" signs posted on those trails and wrecked the prepared trails with abandon.

Compared to nighttime snowmobilers, daytime snowmobilers were geniuses. Hack had a hard time resisting grim satisfaction anytime he learned from the news that another nighttimer had killed himself hitting a rock or tree root lurking under new snow. Overconfidence could kill a snowmobiler, and overconfidence soaked in booze or dope almost always did.

Now some brainless night-timer was disturbing the peace of Hack's new wilderness sanctuary.

Hack was about to yell at the idiot when it struck him that an idiot was not the worst possibility. Just in case, he crouched and slid feet first all the way into his log.

He heard the snowmobile pull to a stop. The driver turned off the engine. He heard the familiar crunch of boots in the snow as the driver trampled around.

"Wilder!" Amalki shouted. "I know you're here. You wanted to meet. So come on out."

Hack heard the crackling of broken branches as Amalki stepped on them.

"I've studied you. You like to ski. I came late for our date and then had no trouble following your tracks. Since the trail stops here, I know you're around somewhere."

Amalki's voice seemed to rise and fall in volume as his search brought him closer to and further from Hack's hiding place.

"It was your skiing that gave me the idea. I bet you never thought you'd meet a jihadi on a snowmobile. But we adapt. You Khaffir invent the technologies and we use those technologies to conquer you. If I believed in irony, I suppose I would find that ironic."

The deafening blast of a gunshot echoed. Hack barely suppressed his startle reflex. Amalki said, "Just wanted you to know I came better prepared for this encounter. Which will be our last."

More crunching of snow and branches.

"Too bad about your friend Amir. Natural for a heretic to take the Khaffir side. And here's another even more delicious irony: I used your knife on him. I saw your caption and I couldn't help myself, "In Emergency Break Glass.""

Amalki was just warming up. "I know you had a wife and you lost her. I've even met her. Did you know that? Probably not. Maybe I'll get the chance to fuck her. If she likes. Or even if she doesn't like."

It was obvious to Hack that Amalki was trying to provoke him into revealing where he was. And the longer Hack held out, the worse the provocation would get.

It was also obvious Amalki meant every threat he made.

"And of course. The most delicious irony of all. A kind of cosmic symbolic irony. Your daughter. Sarai's her name, right? Did you know she's exactly the same age Aisha was when the Prophet consummated their marriage?"

Hack took the deepest breath he could and consciously relaxed every set of muscles one by one. He took another deep breath. And another.

"And I learned just tonight your wife and daughter are both Jews. You should have known better than to marry one Jew and then spawn another one. Especially in our age when the Army of Mohammed is returning to Khaybar. Not Khaybar, Arabia, but Khaybar, Minnesota. Who could imagine such a thing? Only us—the Prophet and his followers."

The crunch of boots seemed to diminish. Was Amalki walking away? There was a pause, then a rustling sound as if Amalki was taking something out of a bag, then the sound of plastic case snapping open.

Amalki said, "I suppose you know what an infrared heat sensor is. It turns out they're cheap around here. Hunters use them to find game. Seems like cheating to me, but…"

"Wouldn't you know that the Prophet anticipated this very situation? He promised, "The Hour will not begin until you fight the Jews, until a Jew will hide behind a rock or a tree, and the rock or tree will say: 'O Muslim, O slave of Allah, here is a Jew behind me; come and kill him.' "The Prophet foresaw this very moment—the trees and rocks giving up their secrets to this device I'm holding."

Hack stifled his groan and clamped his jaw tight. Would his old porous log shield his heat signature from the sensor? Hack had no idea. If the sensor was a cheap model, maybe…?

The crunch of Amalki's boot steps were now the loudest they had been. Then they stopped. Hack heard the man's breathing. He couldn't have been more than eight or ten feet away.

The steps receded again. Then they approached. Then back to loud…then quiet…

Fifty-fifty. If Amalki's boot steps were receding it meant he was walking and facing away. Hack had a chance. With all the dexterity Hack could muster, he grabbed the end of the log with both hands and scooted himself out.

All around Hack, the snow reflected the silver light of a full moon.

Amalki was walking away, pointing his heat sensor at a clump of bushes.

Hack picked up a single ski pole and rushed. He lowered the pole to his right side and held it like a medieval knight's lance, his left hand at its middle to steady and aim the thing. He caught sight of a huge bulge in the left side of Amalki's ski cap. Of course. The wounded ear.

The things you notice when adrenalin slows time down.

Amalki's ear made a handy target. Hack adjusted his lance a few inches up and left and aimed for the bulge.

Amalki heard Hack coming and started to turn. The tip of Hack's hard lance hit square on his ear and popped the bandage and dressing off

Amalki's head. They flew up and to the left.

Amalki shrieked as Hack's momentum took him past. Hack staggered sideways from the shock of the collision and and fell face first into the snow. He scrambled up and turned to face Amalki. Blood dripped from Amalki's head. The pistol lay black in the now at least a dozen feet away from both of them, the heat sensor near it.

Amalki drew his knife. Hack felt for his Kabar and grabbed it out of his coat pocket. He held it blade down and point forward.

Neither spoke. They circled around each other. Amalki was twisting his blade around in an elliptical motion—some sort of knife-fighting technique.

Bad news. Hack knew nothing about knife fighting.

They circled some more. Amalki's knife fighting moves were identical to his slick and sinuous dancing moves. Maybe a mistake. They weren't gliding around on the smooth reliable floor of the Madhouse or Mrs. Malkin's porch. They were on winter wilderness ground. Icy patches and rocks and holes lurked everywhere. Hack lifted and lowered his boots like a robot—straight up and down—the only sure way he knew to keep his footing if he hit ice or other bad footing.

Amalki sneered at Hack's lumbering clumsiness—a Khaffir bumpkin ripe for beheading.

Hack circled and hoped for his chance. It came when Amalki stepped with too much confidence towards Hack and placed his front foot on the slick crown of a snow-topped rock. Amalki slipped off it to his side and bent down on one knee in the snow.

Hack launched himself forward in the air, head down and knife point first. His left shoulder hit Amalki mid-torso and bowled him over, Hack on top. Amalki's curse and groan came simultaneous with the rending noise of Hack's Kabar as it cut deep through Amalki's coat into the soft boneless flesh above his solar plexus and below his ribcage.

Hack lay in terror on top of the now motionless Amalki. Hack's right hand still clutched the Kabar. Hack realized he'd closed his eyes when he dove—like a kid making his first plunge into the deep end of the pool.

Hack waited to die. Nothing happened. Hack opened his eyes. Amalki's face was only a few inches from his own. Like Hal, he stared up at nothing.

Amalki and Hal—brothers in death.

Amalki's blood was pumping out in ever weaker pulses. Then it stopped. Hack felt the wetness on his own chest.

Hack let go of the Kabar and rolled off Amalki and lay on his back and stared up at the heavens. The clouds were gone. The clear black wilderness sky shone with a billion winter stars. The big white moon shown full. A perfect Minnesota January night.

He didn't feel stabbed. But how did he know? He took off his mittens and ran his bare hands over his body. No rips in his coat or pants. All the wetness came from Amalki.

Hack hoisted himself up. Amalki's corpse was an ugly sight. Hack walked over and picked up his ski pole. More ugliness. He didn't want to clean off the gore with his mittens or his hands. He took a few steps away and stuck the pole into a snow bank. He plunged the pole and pulled it out a dozen times. Then another dozen. He stopped only when the gray metal shone pure and clean as new. Then he plunged and pulled another dozen times.

The tip of the pole was clean, but what about Hack's soul? How did he feel? He had just done the unimaginable. He had killed a man. The first man he had ever killed.

Hack considered what he knew about killing, which came mostly from movies. In just about every Hollywood movie the good and decent hero who killed for the first time vomited or uttered words of shame and confusion and wondered what life and death were all about. At the very least the horrific event would trigger a lifetime of deep feelings of remorse or regret.

In this moment at least, Hack felt absolutely no remorse or regret. Did this mean he was not a good and decent man?

He doubted that. It probably just meant that this was one more time Hollywood got everything wrong.

The more he reflected, the more he realized he felt fine. Good even. Positively giddy. The bloody dog was dead. And Hack had killed him. A definite good deed. He flashed on something Sam Lapidos had told him years ago. Jews call a good deed a "mitzvah."

A mitzvah could be any good deed—a favor for a friend, returning someone's lost wallet, feeding the hungry—the list was endless.

Killing Amalki felt to Hack like a definite mitzvah. Maybe the first decent mitzvah Hack had managed in at least three years.

But Sam had also cautioned Hack that mitzvahs sometimes brought complications—for example, unintended consequences.

Hack saw what Sam meant—Amalki's body. Heroes of Hollywood adventures scattered behind them piles of corpses no one seemed to notice. No one ever had to clean up after a Hollywood hero.

Another lie. Hack had to do something about the body. He'd have to to clean up after himself.

Hack walked over and picked up the pistol. A semi-automatic something like his dad's Marine pistol. He stuck it in his coat pocket.

Hack bent over Amalki's corpse. Hack rifled through Amalki's pockets and took everything he found over by the snowmobile and laid it on the ground. He retrieved the heat sensor and piled it there too. Then he went back and cut away and stripped the corpse of all garments including the socks and boots. He carried them over and laid them onto the same ever bigger pile. He got his own gear from the log and brought that over as well and made a separate pile. Anything with blood on it he wrapped in thin tent material from the Gus Go Bag. Then he packed everything in two separate bunches in the snowmobile's storage space.

It took him about thirty minutes to police the entire area.

Finished with that, he indulged his curiosity and examined Amalki's ear. Strange, but he felt no squeamishness, only a kind of clinical curiosity, like a jaded medical examiner. Less than a third of the ear remained to heal. Someone had stitched the purple and green remnant. Must have been agony for Amalki. Good. Good for Mattie.

Now, the body—what to do with it?

Hack sat astride the snowmobile to think. The winter earth was frozen too hard for a burial. Could he hide the body somewhere? Where? Someone would discover it. Then what?

Hack heard a rustling sound in the bushes. He peered over and thought he glimpsed a canine snout.

A wolf. No, two wolves. The lovers from the other night? Attracted by the smell of fresh blood?

"Hi there," he said. "You hungry?"

He held up the pistol for them to see. He had no idea whether wolves could recognize a pistol. He knew they were supposed to be shy about attacking people. But just in case, he was alerting them he was not on the menu.

"I suppose it's been a tough winter," he said. "At least since last week's blizzard. So let's be friends. One hand washes the other. Tit for tat. You scratch my back and I scratch yours. Flesh of my flesh, bone of my bone. You go your way I go mine."

A big wolf emerged from the bushes and sat on his haunches and curled his tail around his front feet. He tilted his huge gray head and inspected Hack in silence. He showed no fear—only curiosity. He gave the illusion he was nothing more than a big friendly harmless dog. But out here he was boss of the night and he knew it.

Hack started up the snowmobile. He saw movement in the bushes as one or more animals startled at the noise and disappeared further out of sight.

The boss wolf never budged. He continued to sit and regard Hack, like a polite neighbor.

Hack took the hint and drove the snowmobile about fifty yards and stopped. He looked over his shoulder and saw only the pink flesh of the naked corpse in the white snow and the big motionless wolf keeping his eyes on Hack.

Hack drove another fifty yards or so and stopped and looked back again.

In the light of the full moon on the snow Hack made out low

shadows slinking from the brush towards the corpse. Maybe eight or ten gathered around it. Some were definitely smaller—cubs. The big one got up and strolled over to the body to take his rightful first bite.

Hack put the machine into gear and drove back towards his Fox.

It felt good feeding the hungry.

Just one mitzvah after another.

29 *The Ogre Again*

At ten A.M. the next morning Hack was sitting in a booth in a café on Shepard Road in St. Paul, wondering how to find Khaled. Hack wore a Twins cap down low over his eyes while he nursed his eggs, toast and coffee and watched ZNN on the TV hung high on the wall behind the lunch counter.

He had spent most of his early morning hours taking his Fox on a winding path to St. Paul, stopping off here and there to distribute various Amalki items onto various frozen dumps. He burned the bloody clothing in a black barrel in one of the dumps.

He broke the gun into parts and distributed its parts along with everything else in the various dumps. He didn't know whom Amalki had killed with it and didn't want to be caught with it on him.

The snowmobile was his biggest challenge. Lacking any better ideas, he had simply washed it with snow as well as he could and left it half a mile down Highway 15 from Childress. It seemed likely Amalki had stolen the snowmobile anyway, so it would be hard to connect with Hack. Hack considered and rejected the idea of setting it on fire. Too much attention.

ZNN still focused on Hack as the monster of the moment. For the entire hour Hack sat there, ZNN coverage was all Hack all the time: his miserable life, his nasty hatreds and his ever-more-abundant murders.

It turned out Hack had killed not only Ahmed Abadi and Amir, but also Hal. The accusation should have come as no surprise, since Hal had been wearing Hack's clothes. Somehow this lie ticked him off even more than the others. He couldn't put his finger on why.

Hack also caught a local news break with an item about an actor named Jack Henderson who had committed suicide.

No mention of Mattie.

Now the younger woman reporter Lauren was interviewing the former F.B.I. Profiler and serial killer expert Dr. Somerset Malmo.

According to Malmo, Hack was engaged in a typical serial killer behavior he called "learning." Hack was adjusting his technique. The more Hack killed, the better he got. He was sublimating his rage better and thereby becoming more effective and more efficient. Of course, his aberrant behaviors all stemmed from the rural male supremacist culture in which he had grown to manhood. Hack's was an upbringing that nurtured and encouraged overbearing masculinity and its corollary admixture of toxic white privilege.

"Wilder is becoming more and more dangerous each time he kills," Dr. Malmo explained. "He has learned he does not need to behead his victim completely to get the satisfaction he craves. With the unfortunate homeless man, a simple plunge of the blade to the chest did it for him. So he is now quicker and therefore even more deadly."

Hack muttered, "The homeless man had a name. It was Hal." Had Hack said it out loud? The few other customers were ignoring him. It occurred to Hack he himself didn't know Hal's last name—so how was he so very much better than this TV clown?

Lauren asked Malmo, "Isn't it possible Wilder was just in a hurry?"

"I don't know about that."

"Maybe he didn't have time to do the complete job he planned?"

Dr. Malmo sighed the condescending sigh natural to officious expertise. "Of course, anything is possible. But I assure you that is not what happened here. This is a textbook case. He is simplifying his ceremony. He is learning how to be a better serial killer the same way a baseball person learns to bat the ball better as he practices more."

The analogy apparently pleased Malmo, because he worked it some more. "Let's say his swing is becoming more compact. And afterwards he is getting harder to catch on the bases."

"That much seems clear," she said. Maybe the man's patronizing tone caused it, but a bit of dryness crept into Lauren's voice. For a fleeting instant, Hack almost didn't despise her. "They haven't caught him so far. Considering they know his name and his face and everything else down to his shoe size, some observers see that as disappointing."

"Well, in defense of my former colleagues, I feel compelled to point out it's only been four days."

Lauren said, "I don't know if Ojibwa City's population has actually doubled with all the local and federal law enforcement, but it could be close."

"Of course, the search area is much bigger than the town—an entire rural region of the state, vast and almost empty."

Lauren shook her head and turned to the camera. "In fact, for more perspective on what increasing numbers of observers are calling a floundering manhunt, we turn to today's F.B.I. news conference happening live. Here is Agent in Charge Blanding at the State Capitol."

Hack dumped more than enough cash on the table and walked out.

He stepped to the side of the cafe. In his pack he found another of his diminishing supply of Gus burner phones and turned it on. Thirty percent—cool. He dialed Sam Lapidos.

Sam answered immediately.

Hack said, "This is Rocky."

"Of course. Hi. About that January picnic. Great idea. It'll be fun."

"Sure." Hack turned off the phone. He walked around to the back of the café and saw a standard black restaurant garbage bin with its lid up. He balanced the phone on the edge of the bin opening and slammed the lid down three times and pushed the pieces of the phone into the bin.

He turned around to head back to his Fox. A man wearing a white apron stood smoking a cigarette just outside the back door of the café. The man gave Hack a speculative look.

Hack shrugged. "Girlfriend. Sick of her and her bitching."

The man gave a sage nod and took a deep drag.

Hack strolled back to his Fox and started it up and headed to Mears Park in downtown St. Paul.

Hack headed for Mears Park because on a mutual dare seven years previous the entire local family had rendezvoused there for a fun traditional Minnesota January picnic. Hack, Lily, Sam, baby Sarai and

Lily's since deceased mother Bea.

The Park itself was one block square in downtown St. Paul. Hack parked near the spot by the river he had used the day before and walked from there to the park in about twenty minutes. He stood around in the park, stamping his feet and hugging himself like the other winter vagrants.

Another twenty minutes passed. A young black man in a heavy coat and gloves approached. He was strikingly large and handsome. In an African sounding accent, he said, "You the gentleman like picnics?"

Hack felt a bit ridiculous, but he played along. "Especially in January."

The man smiled. "My favorite too. I'm Laghdaf. Sam's friend. You will come with me, please?"

"Glad to." Hack followed the man to an old green Toyota Corolla parked nearby. Laghdaf smiled again and opened the passenger door and Hack got in.

Hack said, "Drive me to my own car, please."

"That is my plan," Laghdaf said.

Hack directed Laghdaf on the five-minute drive to the Fox. Laghdaf pulled over to an empty spot in front of it. "You will follow me, please?"

"A pleasure." Hack got into the Fox and followed Laghdaf down to Shepard Road and along it. They exited onto West Seventh and soon after took a right. They drove down two more blocks and Laghdaf stopped his car. He opened the window and pointed to a modest older light blue house set back from the street. He said, "I hope you enjoyed our journey together."

"I did. Thanks."

"A genuine pleasure." And Laghdaf drove away. Hack walked up the front sidewalk of the house. The sidewalk took him past the front of the house and along the left side, where he saw a door. He stepped up onto the small stoop and knocked.

The door opened. Sam said, "Come on in, Nat."

30 A Timely Meeting

"This way," Sam said, and led Hack into a small room off to the side. He closed the room's door and turned to face Hack. "You understand my job?"

"I'm not sure what you're asking."

"My client is Gus."

"I know that."

"After due diligence, I've determined that for the time being I can represent both you and Gus without a conflict of interest."

"Good to know."

"So do you want me for your lawyer? Now's the time."

This was a new Sam Lapidos. Hack had known Sam only as his amiable father-in-law and Sarai's over-indulgent grandfather. But Sam had replaced his usual affable expression with one serious and intense. His eyes glittered. He had his game face on.

Hack thought back to Mattie's ceiling and wondered, owl or hawk? Or both—a hybrid? In any case, a raptor—a fighter. "I'd love to have you for my lawyer, Sam."

"Smart move. Here's my first advice as your attorney. Turn yourself in."

Hack shook his head. "No way."

"Nat, it's essential."

"I've been watching. They're out to get me."

Sam spoke in a soft voice. "Yes, Nat, they are out to get you. But they're less likely to get you with me at your side. Way less."

Hack shook his head again.

"Nat, if you don't, they'll just find you and shoot you and bury you. No one will ever know the truth. Sarai will never know the truth."

"Sarai knows I didn't kill anyone." Then Hack remembered that since the last time he'd spoken with Sarai he actually had killed someone.

"Nat, this is your only way out. And I can't represent you if you don't follow my advice. On this point most of all."

"Sounds like blackmail."

Sam offered a thin smile. "Because it is."

"Okay," Hack said, "On one condition."

"What's that?"

"I talk with Sarai first. And not in jail. As a free man."

"That's hard to guarantee."

"She's my daughter."

"I understand, but—"

"And your granddaughter. And your granddaughter needs to hear it direct from her father. Otherwise, I'm out the door right now and I take my chances."

"Now who's the blackmailer?"

"Me."

Sam studied him. "Something's happened with you, Nat. You're tougher? Meaner? More tenacious?"

"Maybe."

Sam granted him a small smile. "Tough times ahead, Soldier. But I think you'll do fine."

"Can you arrange it?"

"I see a way it could happen. Doesn't depend just on me. Come on." Sam went to the door and opened it and led Hack through a hallway to a small sitting room towards the back of the house.

Where LG and Mattie sat together on a big green couch.

On seeing Hack, LG jumped up and crushed him in his huge arms. Hack looked past LG's shoulder to Mattie, who sat wearing an uncharacteristic shy smile.

Hack said, "Mattie. You got nothing for me?"

She stood and reached out with her left hand towards his right arm. He grabbed her hand in his.

Hack said, "You all right?"

She nodded.

He squeezed her hand and said, "LG. That's enough. I need to breathe."

LG released him and stepped back, beaming.

Sam spoke to the corner of the room. "He's agreed to turn himself in."

"That's a start," Lily said. She stood in the corner leaning against the wall with her arms folded. Her legs were also crossed in a scissors posture. She stared at Hack with a challenging expression.

"We meet again," Hack said.

"Nat."

"There's a condition," Hack told her.

"I didn't agree to any conditions," Lily said.

"In good time," Sam said. "Everybody sit."

Mattie plopped down on the couch. Hack sat next to her. He felt the warmth of her hips against his. LG took a big armchair.

Lily stayed with her wall. Sam gave her a quick glance and took the remaining arm chair. He perched on its edge and leaned forward as if about to speak.

Hack didn't give him the chance. He said to Mattie, "When I saw the blood in your house, I was scared out of my mind."

"Not my blood."

"Whose?"

"That creep from the Madhouse that night. Amalki. Dropped by. Got very physical. And he wasn't fooling around. I'm glad you asked me about him. I was ready for him."

"Did you do something to his ear?"

"How'd you know about that?"

"I happened to run into him. Had a huge bandage over his ear."

From her corner, Lily said, "Is that the same man? With the bandage over his ear? Tariq introduced him as Tayeb something."

"Over where his ear used to be, you mean." Mattie said. "Saw a chunk of it fly off. Then the big baby hugged his head with both hands and started bawling like a spoiled little girl. I grabbed my chance and took off and drove out to the Dropo House. LG spotted me there."

Lily said only, "My," and glanced at Hack as if to ask, this is your new friend?

Sam put in. "And Nat, I found Mattie with LG in the shack you told me about."

"Did your Testoni Norvogese make it through?" Hack asked.

"I've got other shoes," Sam said. "I know you want to catch up, but right now we have more immediate problems."

Hack said, "Not till you tell me what happened with the arson."

"What arson?" Lily asked.

"Last night in the basement of the MinneCentre," Hack said. "When people were still coming in for the concert upstairs. Someone tried to ignite a fire with cell phones and rags. Your pal Amalki/Tayeoub actually. That's how—" Hack paused.

"That's how what?" Sam asked.

Hack wasn't eager to reveal all his dealings with Amalki and their fatal conclusion. "That's how I knew to call you."

Sam said, "The fire was bogus anyway. Set up to fail."

"For what?" Hack asked.

"Hate crime hoax, I think. They wanted it to look like somebody was trying to wreck "Rock The Unity." They didn't necessarily want anyone hurt just yet, although that wouldn't have bothered them any."

Hack said, "I saw on the news that actor Jack Henderson killed himself. You think he did it?"

Sam said, "Maybe. More likely he was a patsy and they killed him to clean up."

"I have a hard time believing any of this," Lily said. "Dad, you working up another of your alternate suspect theories? Something for Nat's defense?"

Sam spoke in the calm even tones of a long patient father. "The fire is no theory, Lily. It's a fact. Like the murders. It's what happened. And more will happen if someone doesn't stop it. And sad to say it doesn't seem like this time it'll be the feds."

Lily glared at her father. Sam maintained his bland paternal expression. Mattie and LG exchanged glances. There was a brief silence.

Hack broke it. "Sam doesn't need to work up anything. I know for a fact there was supposed to be a fire because I stopped it. And I know for a fact your client Tariq's buddy Ear Boy set it up."

"And you know that how?"

"The point is, I stopped it. Then I told Sam about it. And now he's telling you."

Mattie and LG had sat silent. Now Mattie spoke up. "Ms. Lapidos"—

"Call me Lily."

"Okay, Lily, how did I know about the ear? How did Nat? How did you? It's all the same guy with the same ear. It has to be."

Lily tilted her head in apparent thought. "You've got a point, I suppose."

Mattie smiled over at Hack.

Sam said, "Don't forget that first murder. The man Ahmed Abadi."

"How does that fit in?" Hack asked.

Sam said, "Ask Lily."

Lily said, "Sam has very persuasively reminded me that the medical examiner fixed Ahmed Abadi's time of death on exactly the same Friday afternoon I was sitting in Barry's Grill listening to you whine about the divorce."

Hack said. "That's right—I didn't make that connection."

Lily continued, "And since M.O. is the element that ties the murder of Amir to the murder of Abadi, it's reasonable to consider the possibility that since you couldn't possibly have done the Abadi murder you also might not have done the others."

"As I told you," Hack reminded her.

Sam added, "And as Lily should tell the police."

Lily said, "But I did. I told them Nat was with me that afternoon."

Sam said, "And on TV they go right on blaming Hack anyway."

Hack said, "See a pattern, Lily?"

Mattie asked, "Don't you trust him, Lily? You were married to him for ten years. Didn't you learn anything about him?"

Lily gave a small shrug. "Except for that one big lie about quitting his job, he's generally been reasonably honest for a man. But a giant terrorist conspiracy is hard to swallow."

Hack asked Lily, "Did you get in that elevator?"

"What elevator?"

"You know what elevator."

Lily said, "What are you smirking about?"

"Have I got a good reason to smirk?"

"You've never had trouble finding one."

"The elevator last night. When I called you. Did you get on that elevator with Ear Boy?"

"What difference does that make?"

Hack knew all Lily's moves, including her weaselly ones, which he now spotted as she shifted her position against the wall and pulled her folded arms tighter to her chest. In triumph: "You didn't get on that elevator, did you?"

"So what?"

"You trusted me, didn't you?"

"Don't make too much of it."

"What it came down to something really important like Sarai's safety you took my word." Hack folded his own arms and leaned back in triumph.

Sam said, "Now that's something interesting I didn't know. And since we're all one big happy family again, I'd like to move ahead—finally."

Lily shrugged acquiescence. Hack took a deep breath and a sweet moment to revel in the feeling of Mattie warm and safe and alive and leaning against him on the couch.

LG said, "That's all fine. But what about my Dad?"

31 On The Road

"Thanks, LG," Sam said. Then to everyone, "LG gave me Nat's documents off his laptop. I've already given them to my expert and the expert quickly identified a couple of items off the list on that second document."

"I said it was a list," LG said. "Remember?"

Sam smiled at LG. "That's right."

Lily asked, "List of what?"

LG answered, "Things they need."

Sam said, "For example, a heat sensor. Not sure why."

Hack knew why.

Sam said, "And an E.M.P.. I didn't know this, but that stands for Electromagnetic Pulse Generator. It's easy to see why high-tech items like these would be hard to translate. The E.M.P. does what the name says. It generates an electromagnetic pulse. The model listed is a new portable version. Hand held."

Lily asked, "What's it for?"

LG said, "Messing up electronics."

Sam nodded. "Exactly. For example, police can use it to stop fleeing suspects. The pulse interferes with the electronic components of the automobile and the automobile grinds to a stop."

"Anything else?"

"Those two are what we got so far."

Hack asked, "How does 'Toe Lip' fit in?"

"He doesn't know," Lily put in from her wall. "As far as I'm concerned, this is still just his paranoid Islamophobic fantasy."

Hack asked, "Is it a fantasy that Amir and Hal are dead?"

She squared herself towards Hack. "Okay, Dad's got me listening. Now's your chance. Convince me."

Hack told it from beginning to end: the salvaged computers; the Khaybar document and Amir's promise to check it out; Hack's night in the woods while Amir was murdered; Hack's time hiding out at Mattie's house—minus a few private details; his second night in the woods; LG's discoveries on the laptop; what Hack saw and heard at the Department of Mideast Studies, including the Arabic language *Mein Kampf*; Amalki and Khaled murdering Hal; what Hack overheard at the concert; and the fake arson in the basement. He left out the wolves, as well as Amalki's sudden ascent to paradise.

Telling the story took him a half hour.

LG said, "Wow."

Mattie squeezed Hack's hand. "See? A soldier."

"That's quite a tale," Sam said. "But it has the ring of truth and if fits all the evidence I know so far. I'll be proud to help you tell it to the jury. If you testify."

Lily sighed. "Suppose I say that for the sake of argument, I assume your tale is mostly true—assuming also you turn yourself in."

"I am," Hack said. "I will."

Lily walked over to the couch and plopped herself down next to Hack on the side opposite from Mattie. "For the sake of argument," she said to everyone. "Assuming." She folded her arms again.

"Good enough for now," Sam said. "But my daughter is right. 'Toe Lip' is our big mystery right now."

"You've tried translating it back into Arabic?" Hack asked.

"Yes. My expert says the phrase has no cultural or religious or historic significance. It must be a bad translation of something else."

"From what language?" LG asked.

"Well, they assumed English. But that's a good question."

"How about two languages?" LG asked. "Like from one language to another language to a third language?"

Sam looked at LG with growing respect. "I'll suggest that to my expert." Sam turned to Hack. "Nat, repeat again that conversation you overheard on campus."

"You mean Khaled and Amalki?"

"Right."

"Well…they were ragging on each other's Arabic, they talked

about someone they called "The Mujahid"—I'm assuming that's Tariq—and mentioned something they called 'TBS'.

"The TV network?" Mattie asked.

Hack said, "Those are the letters, but they were talking about something else. A translation from some language they hated. One guy—don't remember which—said he didn't know it—the language. The other guy did, but he said he refuses to speak it. Said it was the language of apes and pigs."

"There you go, LG," Sam said. "You're right again."

"What am I right about?"

"Apes and pigs is what some of these people call Jews," Sam said. "The language of apes and pigs is the language of Jews. Hebrew."

"So 'Toe Lip' is Hebrew?" Mattie asked.

"No," LG said. "Something translated into Hebrew or from it. From English or Arabic or both."

"Well, Dad," Lily said. "You know some Hebrew. What does it mean to you?"

Sam said to her, "Finally wish you'd paid attention in Hebrew School?"

"Let's skip that argument, please," Lily said.

"I'll go back to my experts," Sam said. "In the meantime…" He raised his eyebrows at Hack. "Well, Nat? Ready?"

Hack felt Mattie's hand clutch his bicep in a grip of steel. He asked, "Don't forget my condition."

"What condition?" Lily asked from the other side of him.

Sam said, "Nat will turn himself in after he can explain it in person to Sarai. He wants Sarai to see him in person one more time outside of jail."

"In case I never get out again," Hack said.

"And I actually agree with him," Sam said. "We've got to be fair to Sarai too."

"I'll turn myself in right after that," Hack said.

Sam added, "Six P.M. tonight. Sharp. I'll meet you at Mears Park and we'll go in together."

Lily leapt from the couch. She paced across the room and whirled to face all the others. Her eyes glowed with tears. "I've got a condition too," she said. "I want to be there with my baby when you explain to her that her daddy's going to be locked up in jail."

Hack said, "Fair enough."

"Right," Lily said. "Damned right."

"I said right, okay? So where is she?"

"The Jewish Community Center." Lily said.

"Why not school?" Hack asked.

"The JCC's having a party for the kids. For Tu BiShvat."

"Yeah. She mentioned it. We'll take the Fox," Hack said. "We'll talk with Sarai and then I'll leave you there and head over to meet Sam at Mears Park."

Hack stood. LG rose and gave him an awkward hug. Sam took his phone out of his pocket and dialed someone and was already talking into it as he walked into the next room. Mattie stayed on the couch and stared away from everybody into a corner. When he made a move to touch her cheek she pushed his hand away and shook her head.

Hack said to Lily, "Let's go."

Lily glanced down at Mattie and then at Hack but said nothing.

Hack and Lily went out to the Fox. He took the driver's seat and she got in on the passenger side. He started up the car and moved it onto the street. The drive began in silence. For the first few blocks, they both stared straight ahead. It was the first time in eighteen months they had ridden together in a car.

"It's over by Seventh Street," she said. "St. Paul Avenue."

"I know where it is."

More silence.

Then she said, "You know, I always thought you were a wonderful father."

""Yep. I got it all. Wonderful father. Skilled technical professional. Mass murdering spree killer."

"I never thought you killed anyone."

Wrong again, he thought. But he said, "You forget I heard you shooting the breeze with the real murderers at the concert you organized for their benefit."

"That's what you get for eavesdropping,' she said.

"Yep. That's me. Mass murdering eavesdropper."

"Please stop it. I'm trying to apologize. You could too."

"Me? For what?"

Another silence. Then she said, "So I'll begin. I'm sorry. I'm really sorry. I'm totally completely sorry."

"For the divorce?"

"No, the divorce was the right decision. For the way I failed to defend you yesterday. That was wrong."

"Apology accepted."

"So what about you?"

"What about me?"

They were approaching the intersection of Lexington. He said, "Funny to be driving right in this exact moment by the house we shared all those years—just a block away."

"It's a great house. Thanks for letting me keep it."

"I've driven this way so many times I had to stop myself just now from turning by habit and driving right to it."

"I know what you mean," Lily said. "Hey. That might be the JCC bus."

A small yellow school bus was stopped by the right side of the road. Lily said, "Nat. Stop. It is our bus."

Hack pulled over to the side of the road immediately behind the bus.

Lily said, "See. It is ours. They hired one bus to take kids from all the different synagogues and the schools over to the JCC. I know half those kids."

Lily unbelted herself and opened her door and stepped out on the pavement. She turned and leaned back in and said, "Wait here, please. Let me check." She closed her door and walked up along the sidewalk side of the bus

"Nowhere I'm in a hurry to go," Hack said, but she didn't hear him. Hack watched her talk for a few minutes to a heavy-set older woman in a parka, obviously the driver.

Inside the bus was the usual mobile scrum of fifteen or twenty kids taking advantage of the unscheduled stop to run around and laugh and yell and bounce off the inside walls of the bus.

Lily came back to the car and opened the door and got in and closed it again. She put on her seat belt. "The driver said it just stopped. They were driving along smooth as could be and they reached this intersection and the bus just turned itself off and rolled to a stop. She barely managed to glide off to the side of the road in neutral."

"So what now?"

"She's been on the phone. But it'll take at least half an hour before they can roll out another bus to replace this one. When we get to the JCC we can send some parents with a few cars to pick up the kids and take them the rest of the way."

"Sounds like a plan." He started up again and pulled out past the bus. He drove down to Seventh and took a right and headed towards St. Paul Avenue. After a minute or two, he slowed and pulled over to the side of the road and paused there with the engine running.

"What are you doing?"

He checked over his shoulder for oncoming traffic, then gunned the Fox to the left. The wheels squealed as he made a U-Turn. He floored the accelerator and the little engine responded with an agonized roar. The force of the turn threw Lily sideways against her door. "Nat! Stop it!"

"The E.M.P.!" he shouted.

"What?"

"The list! The E.M.P. was on that Khaybar list."

He roared left back up Lexington and nearly skidded off the road to the right and then straightened his path.

He shouted, "Don't you get it? It stops cars!"

The Fox roared up Lexington back to the bus, its engine groaning in pain. A hundred yards ahead Hack saw a man standing by a car parked

195

across from the bus.

As Hack closed in he recognized Khaled. Hack smashed his left forearm down on the horn. It blared and Khaled looked Hack's way. Khaled reached through the driver window of his own car and yanked out a small yellow and gray device like a large taser. He pointed it at the Fox. Khaled pressed down on top of the thing and then pressed again.

Hack slowed down just enough to make sure he could control the Fox and then aimed for Khaled. As he closed in, Hack saw a sequence of expressions flash across Khaled's face—first frustration and then surprise and then terror as Hack roared towards him.

At the final instant Khaled hurled his E.M.P. one way and dove the other. He almost made it. The right front headlight of the Fox clipped Khaled's leg and he whirled into the air and flipped over twice and landed flat on his back in a pile of roadside snow by the curb.

Hack pulled the Fox to a stop and shifted to neutral. He pulled up the parking brake and jumped out and ran back to Khaled.

Khaled's eyes were wide in obvious agony. "I can't move. I think you broke my back."

"Your fault. You should have stuck the landing," Hack said. Lily had come up to stand beside him.

She said, "Nat?"

"Yeah."

"I take back that apology. You're crazy. You are some kind of monster. I just saw you. You ran down an innocent man just because—I don't know—just because he looks Muslim or something. And now you're taunting him. You're really the fiend they say." She grabbed her phone out of her purse and punched it with her finger. "I'm calling the cops. Turn yourself in. Right now. It's the only sane thing to do."

"Hang on." Hack leaned down and pulled Khaled's coat open. He saw what he expected to see. He lifted the semi-automatic weapon to show Lily. The nasty short rifle had fit neatly under Khaled's coat with its collapsed stock and a very short barrel. One ugly magazine jutted down.

"That magazine holds thirty rounds," Hack said. He bent down and pawed through Khaled's coat with his left and pulled out another magazine. "This one holds thirty more rounds. You still think I'm a fiend?"

Lily just stared at him and then down at Khaled.

Khaled said, "We thought you were dead."

Hack said, "Mistakes happen. Especially to you."

Khaled said, "The E.M.P. worked on the bus. Why not on your car?"

"You jihadis—still short on American know-how. Should have done your research. The car's a 1973 Audi Fox. A classic. Old style. No electronics to scramble." He turned to Lily. "See? Clunkers have their advantages."

Lily was shivering. She hugged herself. "Don't joke."

Hack touched her shoulder with his fingertips. "You're right. Now I really am sorry."

Hack looked around. The bus driver stood in front of her bus and just stared at him. Children's faces gaped through the bus windows.

A rusty van lumbered down the middle of the road and passed between Hack and the bus. It slowed as if to gawk and then resumed its original speed. The big black letters on its yellow side read "Exterminators." It ran low to the ground as if weighed down by a mass too heavy for its suspension. Something about the black letters on yellow and their vaguely familiar font disturbed Hack. He caught a glimmer in Khaled's eye—something about the man's expression.

"You know that van?" Hack asked.

Khaled looked away.

That by itself increased Hack's suspicions. He leaned down. "You know that van?"

Khaled grunted, "Too late. Doesn't matter now."

Hack said, "I wouldn't count on Amalki. He's off the board."

Khaled said, "I don't believe you."

The wail of sirens rose in the distance.

Lily said, "Nat, you're still going to turn yourself in, right? It's the only sane thing to do."

But Hack stayed on Khaled. "Your career as a jihadi is over. One last chance. Who's driving that van? I promise you it's not Amalki."

Khaled's chest rattled as he expelled his final breath. His eyes turned dull. Another brother in death.

Hack sprinted for the Fox. He paused only to grab the E.M.P. off the street. The Fox was still idling in neutral with its driver door open. He jumped in and slammed the door behind him and released the parking brake and took off.

He knew another way to the JCC. Instead of turning back towards Seventh Street, he drove in the direction he was already pointed and two blocks later made a hard left.

He reached St. Paul Avenue. The JCC Building was on his right. He turned left and drove about fifty yards down St. Paul Avenue towards Seventh Street and saw the yellow van lumbering up the road towards him. The JCC was now behind him. He pulled his Fox over and stopped.

His phone rang.

"Sam, I'm busy right now."

"Won't take long. Figured out 'Toe Lip'."

The van slowed.

"Sam, busy!"

"It's Tu BiShvat! LG was right. It's a three-way translation screwup. I'll explain later. I've called the cops. If you and Lily are already at the JCC warn everybody and do whatever you can."

"On it," Hack said and threw the phone on the floor.

The van continued its sluggish approach. Hack rolled down his window and pointed the E.M.P. at the van and pressed the big top button he hoped was the trigger.

For a moment nothing seemed to happen. Then the van slowed and stopped no more than twenty yards away.

The driver reached down out of Hack's sight and punched and pulled, apparently at various controls, obviously trying to restart. Hack got out of his his car and strolled towards the van.

The driver was pounding the steering wheel. He glanced up and saw Hack and stopped pounding and stepped out of the van onto the street.

It was Daghestani. "You," he said. "The piano player."

"I was just moonlighting. My day job is foiling terrorists."

"They promised they'd killed you. I should have known not to trust those idiots. They're completely unreliable."

"They're also completely dead."

"So you say."

"Amalki didn't show, did he? And he was supposed to drive, right?"

"You seem to know a lot."

"And now you have to do the job yourself."

Daghestani sighed. "Isn't that always the way?"

"Last night I fed Amalki to the wolves. Just now I ran Khaled down like the mutt he was. And you've got about two minutes in dog years yourself till the cops arrive and peek inside that van."

"The van I still have."

"And I still have the E.M.P.."

"This is close enough to the building. I can detonate here."

"No, you can't."

"That's right. As you said, you still have the E.M.P.. It stops all electronics, not just cars. Including electronics to trigger explosives."

Tariq pulled a short curved blade from the inside of his coat. "So I guess I'll have to relieve you of it." He took a step towards Hack.

Hack had opened his big mouth again. Now what? Any beginner could get lucky with a thrust of a ski pole and a dive with a knife. Any teenager could run down a pedestrian with a speeding car. Knife fighting required training. He had none. From Daghestani's footwork as he approached and the way he was shifting the knife in his hands, Daghestani possessed enough training for both of them.

And no ice this time—the street surface was a dry perfectly plowed black asphalt—splendid traction for Daghestani to glide forward and slice Hack like a side of beef.

Hack drew his Kabar anyway. Might as well go down fighting.

More sirens shrieked, this time louder and closer. How about stalling?

Daghestani shuffled closer. Hack backed away. Daghestani approached and Hack backed away some more. And so on. They circled around on the road. Daghestani sneered, "You don't know what you're doing, do you?"

"Not really. But time's running out. Better hurry."

"Right again." Daghestani shifted his blade to his left hand and with his right drew a small black pistol. He aimed it at Hack.

Daghestani stood in the middle of the road facing away from Seventh Street towards Hack and the JCC building behind Hack. Hack saw something Daghestani couldn't see. A tidy black Beamer coming up the road. Hack recognized it as one he'd once driven himself.

Hack said, "Actually, I changed my mind. There's no particular hurry."

"But a hurry nonetheless," Daghestani said.

The BMW engine roared from behind him and he turned. Hack dove away to the right.

Hack didn't see but he heard—the smack of auto hood and fender as it smashed into Daghestani's flesh.

Hack hit the curb hard and felt something give in his left shoulder. Despite his agony he grinned in relief as he turned his head and surveyed the scene.

The BMW had stalled at the side of the road about thirty yards down. The driver door opened. Lily emerged and with great deliberation stepped over to Daghestani lying at the side of the street. She peered down at him for a moment and then walked over to Hack. Her face shone white as paper. Her features were locked in rictus and her eyes seemed to bulge out of her head.

Four squad cars roared up and stopped. Cops jumped out and opened their doors and squatted down behind them, leveling shotguns and pistols at Lily and Hack.

As if mildly curious, Lily swiveled her head in the direction of the cops and then back to Hack.

Hack said, "I knew letting you keep the BMW would pay off."

She said, "I ran to the house and took it and came for Sarai. Then I saw the van and you and Tariq in the street and his gun."

Cops were yelling threats. They wanted Lily and him down on their bellies. Now!

Hack said, "Lily."

"What?"

"Lily. You've got to turn yourself in. It's the only sane thing to do."

Tears flooded her eyes and her shoulders start to quake. He got up and staggered over to her. He heard the cops screaming to stay put but he ignored them. He put his good left arm around her shoulder and she rested her head against him.

Then the cops rushed them and carried them off.

32 A Delayed Tu BiShvat

Two Weeks Later

Hack wanted to put the entire experience behind him, but the people he cared about wouldn't let him. Worse yet, they insisted on watching the news.

Of course the JCC had canceled the official Tu BiShvat celebration. After all Sarai's preparations, Lily didn't want her cheated, so Lily threw a "Better Late Than Never Tu BiShvat Party" at her St. Paul house. She invited Hack and anyone he wanted to bring. He wanted to bring Gus and LG and of course Mattie. He was living at least temporarily at Mattie's house while he decided what to do about his own.

He had visited his home just once to collect clothing and some other personal items. He avoided his basement.

Sam was at Lily's too. It was Sam and Gus who insisted on watching ZNN. They wanted to gloat over their recent courtroom victory. Judge Robinson had thrown out the entire case against Gus. Gus and Sam were already counting their money from the upcoming lawsuit.

Sarai and Mattie sat on the carpet off to one side of the family room. Sarai was explaining her Tu BiShvat Seder Plate. The plate was about twelve inches around. Twelve small piles of various fruits and nuts were seated in twelve small depressions on the plate.

Sarai pointed to each fruit one by one. "Here's dates, and grapes, and there's almonds and figs, and let's see, olives, pomegranates, almonds, carobs, apples, pears and citrons. That's like an old-fashioned orange."

Hack had never seen Mattie glow like she glowed sitting with Sarai. She was smitten. She tracked Sarai's every little movement and listened with deep seriousness to every word. "Does each fruit mean something different?"

"It's all about trees. Everything here comes from a tree. Except the wheat. We count wheat as a fruit."

"Why?"

"Wheat's like the basic requirement for all the others. It gives us strength so we can grow the trees and harvest the fruit."

"I see."

Two nights previous Mattie had sat up straight in bed next to Hack gibbering in terror. He grabbed her by her shoulders and she stared wild-eyed and threw wild punches he mostly blocked before she recognized him and fell into his arms.

"It was that Amalki creep," she said. "He was coming after me again."

"It's okay."

"I flailed at him with a knife and when I cut off that chunk of his ear he just grabbed it off the floor and gobbled it and grinned."

"It's okay."

"And he's still out there. For real. What if they never catch him? What if he comes back?"

"Won't happen."

"How can you be sure?"

"I'm sure."

She laid her face on his chest. "I wish I could be."

So he had to tell her what he'd done to Amalki that moonlit night in the wilderness, if only so she could sleep again. She was the only person he'd told or ever wanted to tell.

At the party, Hack and the others watched Hack's favorite ZNN news team griping about the dismissal of the case against Gus.

The spectrally thin older woman Jane something-or-other and the younger woman Lauren and the black guy with glasses and bow tie—Tad—all sat around the same semicircular desk with its same rounded front.

Jane: "Lauren, what exactly happened at this morning's hearing that led to today's shocking outcome?"

Lauren: "Judge Robinson threw out the case·against Augustus

Albert Dropo."

Jane: "But how could this happen?"

Lauren: "The legal technicalities would confuse viewers unschooled in the law. The bottom line is that Sam Lapidos sprung one of his trademark Sam Lapidos tricks."

Hack had sat in back of the court room and watched the entire hearing. When Sam pulled his "trick" and asked for the speedy trial guaranteed by the Constitution and a bunch of statutes, Judge Robinson asked nicely whether the prosecution was ready to proceed.

The Prosecutor was a tall woman named Page. She stood up and explained the government wasn't ready for trial.

Judge Robinson asked, "Why not?"

"Evidence continues to be gathered."

Judge Robinson spoke in a pleasant tone, as if he were asking Page about her summer vacation. "How can you indict someone if you haven't already gathered the evidence to prove him guilty?"

"Some of what the government initially believed demonstrable has turned out challenging in detail at this time."

"Interesting, if vague. Now, as the Court understands it, you've charged Mr. Dropo with being a co-conspirator, but with whom? Mr. Wilder? But Mr. Wilder has not been charged with any crime. And the state has dropped its accessory charge against Mr. Dropo."

"We're concerned about a possible larger conspiracy, Your Honor. It's clear there was one."

"And what specific action did Mr. Dropo take in furtherance of this conspiracy?"

"Clarifying details of that nature is one reason the government needs additional time. The prosecution does not wish to be premature in its assertions."

Judge Robinson said, "Another interesting statement. Of course, without evidence to back up your assertions, you are by definition premature, if that's the right word. Also, the Court has finally had the opportunity to review the documents the prosecution so reluctantly provided, and it turns out that the prosecution and the F.B.I. willfully failed to provide not only to the defense but to this Court exculpatory evidence—after having displayed egregious lack of candor beforehand."

"There are national security concerns, Your Honor."

"During which time Mr. Dropo languished in jail without bail or the ability to develop an effective defense. Constitutional rights were denied or at least delayed based on the Prosecution's false representations."

"With all due respect, Your Honor, that might be a little unfair."

"If so, only a little. And then it happens that exculpatory documents the government so reluctantly provided this Court turn out to contain nothing whatsoever of any national security interest."

Judge Robinson looked directly at Agent Blanding, who oddly enough had sat right next to Hack in the back row without ever acknowledging him. "It seems no coincidence that most, if not all, of these undisclosed documents were authored by the FBI."

"Your Honor, the Prosecution itself does not have complete access to F.B.I. documents."

"But as you know, you are nonetheless jointly responsible with the F.B.I. for what the F.B.I does and does not do. Otherwise, it's an unwinnable game of hide-the-ball for the defense, isn't it?"

Page stuck to her guns. "Your Honor, is the Court going to impose at this early stage of the proceedings requirements that by rule generally apply only in preparation for trial?"

"Why wait?" Judge Robinson looked out over the court room. "Even if the accused is ultimately exonerated—which based on the available admissible evidence he must be—any further proceedings under these conditions would be unconscionable. This entire case is now tainted beyond remedy by flagrant prosecutorial misconduct. The Court therefore dismisses the case against Mr. Dropo with prejudice."

Hack heard Gus whisper to Sam sitting next to him, "What does that mean?"

Judge Robinson heard Gus too. "Mr. Dropo, it means there will never be a trial in this case. The prosecution against you is over.

Permanently. You're free to go. Hasta La Vista."

But now in its coverage ZNN was leaving out everything Hack had seen and heard with his own eyes and ears.

Jane: "Lauren, does this mean because of legal technicalities no one will be punished for these murders? Not even Nathanael Andrew Wilder, the man ZNN coverage has so thoroughly exposed as an Islamophobe and white supremacist?"

Lauren: "That depends on whether you're one of those right-wing zealots and conspiracy theorists who point their fingers at Tariq Daghestani and Tayeb Chahuan. Of course, Daghestani is dead and Chahuan is missing altogether, so they are not here to defend themselves against these uncorroborated accusations."

Todd: "Once again so many in our community are disappointed. Yet another white man evades accountability for his role in the deaths of people of color. And how many minority defendants have access to the kind of Sam Lapidos legal gymnastics available to Dropo and Wilder? This travesty will further destroy the minimal remaining confidence black folks have in the legal system—if that's possible at this point."

LG shouted, "Hey! What about Tayeb having that computer from Nat's basement in his apartment? With Amir's blood all over it."

Gus said, "And what about the computer from Mattie's house he had? With Hack's and Mattie's DNA. And Tayeb's own blood on Mattie's wall."

Hack barely heard Lily's soft voice. "And who will ever be able to forget Tariq's van load of explosives?"

Lily had lapsed into a subdued melancholy since she saved him that day in the street. But what could Hack expect? She was the kind of good and decent person who would react exactly the way Hollywood thought a person ought to react to killing someone—unlike himself, it turned out.

Lily had also confided to him that she wasn't going to let Sarai see any part of any psychological aftermath of that terrible day. No matter what she might suffer in private, Lily was going to stay a happy and upbeat mother for Sarai.

Sam watched the ZNN coverage in silence. He said, "They got their story and they're sticking to it. But I wonder where that Tayeb fellow went to?" He shot a bland look over at Hack.

Hack offered Sam his best LG teenage shrug.

The doorbell rang. Sam got up and went to answer it. Three more guests. Hack recognized them from times when he'd occasionally joined Lily and Sarai at the synagogue. Nice people.

Gus said to Hack, "I guess we'll have to keep our eyes open for that Amalki dude."

That afternoon, Hack had greeted Gus on the sidewalk when Gus came out of the court building a free man. Neither said anything. They just hugged one of those awkward manly hugs women find annoying.

As they walked together down the street towards the Fox, Hack noticed two young guys and a young woman following them down the street. The three looked about twenty years old.

This went on for three blocks.

Hack said, "I'm sick of this."

"Just ignore them," Gus said.

After two more blocks Hack said, "Enough of this crap," and turned down an alley.

The three followed them into the alley.

About fifty yards in, Hack turned and said, "What's up?"

One of the them had a blond scraggly beard and was as tall as Gus but not nearly so thick. "We just want you to know we're on to you. Both of you."

"On to what?"

The blond guy said, "Don't think you'll get off forever. Anti-fascist justice is coming."

Gus groaned and said, "Let's just leave. I just got out. I'd like a day or two of freedom before I go back in."

Hack said, "You're right," and he turned to leave. He heard one of the three call out "Nazi!"

Hack turned back. "What was that?"

The shorter male with the dark beard said, "Nazi!"

Hack said, "Don't use that word."

The girl said, "Why not? That's what you are. A Nazi." Hack noticed she had a cute round face.

"My grandfather died fighting Nazis."

The blond guy said, "So?"

"So those are fighting words."

The smaller guy said, "We don't mind fighting Nazis."

Gus groaned again.

The smaller guy said, "Imagine how ashamed he'd be of you now."

The girl laughed. "Yeah! His grandson the Nazi."

The other two laughed with her.

This wasn't like with Amalki or with Daghestani—there was no fear and no calculation or logic and no sense of obligation or duty to follow through on an impossible task luck or fate had somehow stuck him with. It was just rage. It boiled up and the world turned first black and then red like in the books and an instant later Hack felt his right fist explode into the big one's jaw. The big one fell and the girl screamed and the smaller guy with the brown beard stood there with a confused look on his face.

Gus said, "Not today. Please!"

Hack said, "Then get me out of here."

Hack felt Gus crush him with both arms around his shoulders and lift him and carry him twenty feet down the sidewalk and then set him down pointed away from the three nitwits. Gus said, "Don't look back."

But Hack heard the girl shout the word "Nazi" again and he turned. The other two were helping the blond guy, who was sitting up with his hands holding his jaw. When the other two saw Hack turn they ditched their friend and ran off. Hack thought they were both crying.

Gus grabbed him again by the shoulders and again faced him away from the three. "I said, don't look back," and this time Hack didn't look back.

After they'd walked a few more minutes, Hack said, "That was a mistake."

"No shit."

Hack rubbed the knuckles of his right hand. "I shouldn't have hit that guy on the hard bone of his jaw. I should have hit him someplace soft like in the solar plexus or in the floating ribs. I might have hurt my hand. I need it for the band. I got us back our gig at the Madhouse. And maybe some other possibilities."

Gus laughed and laughed on and off the entire time the two made their way through the alley and then a few more blocks to the Fox.

Hack took Gus home to his house and to his son and the three conducted a small ceremony in which Hack handed back the Dropo family Kabar and they all enjoyed an ice-cold beer out of Gus's cooler. And then another. Then the three got in the Fox and Hack drove to Sarai's party, stopping only to pick up Mattie as she got off her day waitressing at the restaurant.

In their corner of the Tu BiShvat party, Mattie and Sarai were laughing about something silly that way women and girls do. Hack caught sight of Lily's pleased expression as she watched Mattie and Sarai laughing together. Lily did really have a generous spirit. Hack had told Lily about Mattie's loss of her own daughter.

So much loss. Which of course also reminded him of Amir. Nothing to be done. Amir was gone. Mattie's daughter was gone. Hal was gone.

Hack got up and walked over to where Mattie and Sarai sat on the floor. Mattie reached up to touch his arm with her hand. He squeezed her hand in his.

As if she somehow read Hack's thoughts, Sarai said, "I miss Uncle Amir."

Hack said, "I miss him too."

"Do you think Uncle Amir would have enjoyed Tu BiShvat?"

"I'm sure he would have."

"Mom explained to me our religion is not his."

"He would have enjoyed Tu BiShvat and he would have enjoyed

just being with you. Like he always did. Like Mattie does."

"Yes," Mattie said. "Like me."

"I wish he could."

Hack said, "Me too."

Sarai said, "And Zarah too."

Hack asked, "Zarah?"

"You remember. His daughter. My cousin. Sort of."

"Yes, of course."

Sarai asked, "Do you know where she is?"

"How could I?"

"Could you find out?"

"That'd be very hard, Sarai. I wouldn't know where to begin."

"What if she's in trouble? And with no father to protect her like you and Mom and Amir protected me and the other kids?"

Sam stood nearby chatting with the new guests. Sarai called over to him. "Grandpa?"

Sam glanced over at Hack, eyebrows up in a silent question. Sam shrugged back the equivalent of "Come see for yourself."

Sam stepped over and smiled down at Sarai with obvious adoration. "What is it, sweetheart?"

"I was asking Dad if he could find Zarah."

"Zarah?" Sam asked.

Hack said, "Amir's daughter. From things Amir said Sarai's pretty sure Amir had a daughter named Zarah."

"Not pretty sure, Dad. Sure."

Sam said, "I see."

Sarai continued, "Uncle Amir's daughter is my cousin, right? I think of her that way. And I don't have even one single cousin."

Sam said, "I see."

"Grandpa, Dad says you're the smartest guy he knows."

Sam said, "Well..."

"Dad says you can do anything. Can you find her? Please?"

"Is she missing?"

"I've never gotten to meet her. So she's missing as far as I'm concerned," Sarai explained with impeccable logic.

Sam gestured for Hack to follow him into the most distant corner of the room. As they passed Gus, Hack gave him a head shake to follow. LG joined them.

The three stood in the corner together. Sam said, "What's this all about?"

Hack said, "I just stumbled clueless into something and then blundered my way out of it. Amir knew from the beginning what he risked and did it anyway and it killed him. To protect Sarai and other people he didn't even know."

Sam said, "Understood."

"Now I'm wondering whether I can do any less for his daughter than he did for mine."

Sam said, "You sure she exists?"

"I'm not sure she doesn't."

Sam said, "Sarai's always had her own ways of knowing things."

Hack had never seen Sam turn Sarai down for anything.

So far Gus had said nothing. Hack looked at him. Gus said, "Whatever you want, partner."

LG watched the older men and listened.

Hack thought about all he'd seen and done the past month and looked around the room in dazed wonder. All six of the people he loved most in the world were with him in that room in that moment. All six had their eyes on him: not only Sam and Gus and LG, but Mattie, eyebrows raised in her familiar challenging expression; Lily in one of her favorite stances, arms crossed and her head tilted to the side. And as she always did when she wanted something special from her father, Sarai just smiled at him, her wise child's eyes wide open.

THE END

Author's Afterword

I hope the fact you have gotten this far in this book means that you have enjoyed it.

If so, please feel free to take the time to visit the Amazon.Com web page for "Khaybar, Minnesota" and write a review. Please be constructive and honest. Your review can make a difference for the book and for its author.

In any case, thanks very much for purchasing and reading "Khaybar, Minnesota."

- The Author

Made in the USA
Middletown, DE
10 December 2018